THE DEPTHS
OF
LOYALTY

By

Asher Clark

Dedicated to my mother, who loved to read.

To my children. Anything is possible, so pursue your dreams.

I want to thank Leslie Lehr for her invaluable developmental editing support. Her insight into the plot and characters was crucial to the final story.

Table of Contents

Chapter 1 (May) –
Folly at The Green Dragon Tavern

*W*e *shall be watching for your father's return.* Those dreadful words lingered as I woke at first light, to pounding behind my temples, my mouth dry as old parchment. Just the night before, I was frequenting the Green Dragon Tavern, where not too long ago, the Sons of Liberty once whispered their rebellion over tankards of ale. It was in this very tavern that the likes of Samuel Adams, John Hancock, and Paul Revere conspired, forging plans that would shake a tyrannical empire. Now, their framed silhouette profiles hung on the walls, silently bearing witness to the lesser rebellions that played out nightly within its confines. The Green Dragon Tavern was a place where I felt unmoored, untethered to demands of everyday life. In a way, it was a refuge. A place where I could come and go freely, unburdened from the imposing will of other men's ambitions. But last night, everything began to change.

I was standing near a well-worn oak table, observing a group of men playing the dice game hazard.

"You in or out, lad? Don't stand there gaping all night." one of the men said.

The man's winnings were stacked low. His loose, rolled-sleeve linen shirt under a wool homespun waistcoat and heavy canvas breeches announced his occupation as a longshoreman.

"Just taking it in for the time being."

"Don't tell me you are broke? Or worse…too worried you might lose?"

I contemplated his taunt long and hard. I had success in other gambling affairs many times before: rooster matches, fights and card games, but not hazard. In fact, gambling was how I escaped the clutches of having to be a serf to a life filled with monotonous labor and toil. I fumbled the money in my pocket, the winnings I had compiled over the course of the week.

"I can see you mulling it over. Who knows? You might leave with your pockets heavy," the longshoreman said, glancing at me with a slight smirk.

Those words were enough. I eased into an empty scarred wooden chair, ready to win myself another day unburdened.

"Where've I seen you before?" another man asked.

"He is the son of Ben Thompson, the owner of the Atlantic Shipping Co.," the longshoremen answered.

"That I am," I confirmed as I placed a small bet.

"Ought you be in some counting house squinting at ledgers with those pretty blue eyes of yours?" one sailor jeered.

The men roared with laughter in unison. I let their jibes roll off me since I knew it meant I was welcome at their table.

I was betting on luck, until I could figure out the inner workings of the game. But after a few rounds, luck never turned in my favor. I reached into my pocket where my money once was, yet was now empty. I was shocked with disbelief at how fast I lost every dollar.

"John Lowe will lend you some money if you fancy another chance," the longshoreman said, gesturing towards a table in the corner.

Set on recovering my losses and pride, I strode to the corner where John Lowe sat, looming over the table like the broadside of a ship. Approaching him was a gamble all in itself. A first mate and fisherman by profession, he had a thick frame with refined muscles earned from hauling countless nets and barrels. A sailor's fid made of bone, tapered and sharp, hung on a cord around his belt. His nose was slightly askew while his eyes were small, dark, and sat like black stones deep beneath his thick brows. As for myself, I was nothing like him. Younger. Less scarred by the world. I was fit, but not like him. Not with that sort of brute strength. My nerves began to shake as I stood next to him.

"Caleb, what sum did you have in mind to borrow?" John inquired.

"I was thinking…ten dollars," I replied, hoping he would oblige. I normally avoided borrowing from him. But no one else was around to lend me the credit. So I took the risk.

His cold, impenetrable eyes focused on mine. "Your father…he hasn't been back from his voyage yet, has he?"

"True enough. But he'll be back soon."

"All right, but let me be real clear…it ain't free. There's interest."

"Of course," I replied wearily. I knew exactly what he meant, and it had nothing to do with money.

He reached into his coat, pulled out ten silver pieces of eight, then handed them to me. I walked back to the table, full of determination to get all my money back and more. Taking an interest in my risky venture, a small crowd of sailors and local merchants gathered around the table. Candlelight from sconces flickered, casting our figures in restless, shifting outlines against the walls. I enjoyed moments like these. I often ended up thriving when I was down a hole.

After a few rolls, I began to ride a favorable streak, and my pile of winnings grew alongside my intake of whiskey and ale. Soon enough, I won all my money back. I even had enough to sustain a few more nights of further revelry. A wiser man, or at least a sober one, might have said it was time to quit. But gambling is a creature of momentum. It has its own pulse and its own logic. At that moment, I was convinced the night was mine, so I continued to roll the dice.

On the next turn, I felt the weight of the dice in my palm, letting the moment linger. When I let go, the dice tumbled on the table, the outcome entirely up to fate. But when the dice stopped, my spirit sank, and my anger stirred as my streak had ended abruptly. I continued to play, my streak now turning from winning to losing till everything I had was lost again.

"Lad, you are no good at this game," the longshoreman jabbed.

But I didn't let his jest deter me. Now that I understood how the game worked and tasted victory, I could easily win it all back again. I borrowed more money. Yet, this time, I doubled my initial buy only to lose another round. So I borrowed some more and rolled again, then again, until I lost count. Each round, the stacks of the other players grew higher, while my anger grew more furious.

When I asked John Lowe to borrow more, he looked at me with a terrifying glare, concentrating deep into my soul.

"Save your breath. You even realize how deep in debt you are?"

"I am good to pay back the money. I just need a good streak."

"You're at your limit, foolish boy. You owe a hundred dollars."

Though I desperately wanted to depart in shame, I knew walking away would have been a sign of disrespect.

"Listen well. This debt is not owed to me, but to Mr. Bellamy. You'll have it paid in two weeks. No excuses. Or I'll be sent to collect. Understand?"

"Understood, sir," I replied, dreading the enormous hole I had gotten myself into.

John was sinister in his own right. But it was who he worked for whom I feared the most. Mr. Bellamy, the owner of Bellamy Trading Co., a cod fishing company whom John was employed by, had an even worse reputation. Sanctioned by the Continental Congress during the war, Mr. Bellamy had once been a feared privateer, a man who skirted the line between patriot and marauder. Now, with war far behind him, he dealt in codfish and shipping contracts. A quieter life that, if the rumors were true, no longer satisfied him. Some said he was setting his sights on the West

Indies, where sugar, molasses, and rum promised more adventure and wealth than salted fish.

"Please, John, lend him some more money," the longshoreman yelled from the table, while I stood shamefully.

The men at the table laughed and cheered, their stacks now higher because of my losses.

The low wooden ceiling beams closed in on me as my head spun from a toxic blend of ale and worry. The wooden floor beneath me began to sway, as though I was aboard a ship in the middle of a violent gale. My pockets were empty, any temporary winnings long gone. I managed to gather what strength I had left, stumbling up the basement stairs.

"We'll be watching for your father's return," John's voice carried from the back of the basement, reaching me on the stairs, the seriousness of a death sentence postponed rather than lifted.

I continued up the confined stairs and stepped out into the crisp Boston night. The town had fallen silent, ghostly in its emptiness. There was no clamor from neighborly conversations, nor the rhythmic clatter of horse-drawn carriages on cobblestone-laden streets. I walked along narrow, winding roads, as the shadows closed with each step. I passed shuttered shops and rows of federal-style townhouses with brick facades darkened against the late evening sky. I had not intended to lose such a large amount of money or be in the position where I would have to inform my father of the large gambling debt I had tallied. To my dismay, the tavern was no longer a place I could frequent for the foreseeable future, and my father's imminent return pressed heavily upon my mind.

Chapter 2 (May) –
A Hidden Debt

While I gathered myself from bed, my mother, with the help from my sisters, Charlotte and Alice, orchestrated breakfast below: the mingling scent of cornmeal and biscuits rose in tandem with the shuffle of their happy footsteps. For now, they didn't know what kind of trouble I had gotten myself into. And if I could figure something out quickly, they never would.

Across the bedroom, my younger brother Jameson lay sprawled upon his bed, his fingers lightly gripping the pages of *Robinson Crusoe*, his lips moving faintly as he read. Though often a pest, he was the best sort of brother, sharp of mind and unruly enough to make life interesting. He was a shipwright apprentice, learning hull carpentry at the wharf. At thirteen, he was thin and wiry, with a quiet bravery that belied his size. His crisp white linen shirt, its collar peeking above the neckline of his faded navy waistcoat, had been stitched with care despite its modest origins. As always, his dark brown hair fell in unruly waves, tousled by the wind and salt air, with a single lock that refused to be tamed, slipping over his forehead no matter how often he pushed it back.

"Something bothering you?" Jameson asked, his eyes never leaving the page.

"Just the aftermath of too much fun."

"You lost money gambling, didn't you?"

I snapped a gaze towards him, rubbing at my side. "I didn't lose anything."

"Just tell me. I know you better. Your countenance betrays you. You know I will find out," Jameson said, leaning towards me with a serious look.

Lying to him further was an option, but at that moment, I needed all the allies I could get. Even those who might inform my mother of my painful secret.

"It's nothing," I muttered. "Just…say nothing of it."

He didn't answer right away. He held my gaze for a moment longer, then nodded slowly. But I could see it in his face. He wasn't done pressing me. I waved a hand, unwilling to engage in his self-righteousness so early. I reached beneath my bed to retrieve a small brass pocket compass. I walked over to him and tossed it onto his bed with a soft flick of my wrist.

"Here. This is for you."

He glanced at it, then, without hesitation, abandoned Defoe's marooned Crusoe for his newest amusement.

"A bribe?," he said with a crooked, sarcastic grin.

"It's not, you half-wit," I said with a smirk. "I've had it for a while now."

"Thank you, brother," he replied, still mesmerized by its mechanics. "Where did you get this?"

Before I could answer, I hurried downstairs through the hall where the parlor table was already laden with steaming mush, warm biscuits crowned with butter, and a pitcher of fresh milk. I wanted to indulge and rid myself of my pounding headache. But I dared not risk staying; I had to leave swiftly. Coat in hand, I entered the parlor to grab a biscuit.

"Well, look who's joined the living," Charlotte remarked.

Charlotte was the elder of my younger sisters, a reflection of our mother in looks and not so much in manner. She was, in many ways, perfect—almost too perfect and entirely aware of it.

"How creative," I muttered while walking, ready to slip out the kitchen door before anyone could ask where I was going. But as I made my way into the kitchen, I nearly collided with my mother, her apron dusted with flour, the signs of the morning's labor still fresh upon her.

"Caleb," she said in a questioning tone.

I froze. Her voice was sharp and knowing.

"Join us for breakfast," she said, not asking but demanding.

Without arguing, I made my way back to the parlor and took a seat at the table. My sisters and mother joined me, followed by Jameson soon after.

"You look awful…Where were you last night?" my mother asked.

"You can barely see the blue in his eyes. He was too busy reveling at the tavern again, of course," Alice chimed in, her sharp, high-pitched whine echoing through the kitchen.

"You should have been helping with the ledger before Father gets back," Charlotte reminded everyone.

The family ledger! She had to bring that up. The long hours of entries and balancing accounts made me sick to think about. I had given that endeavor up and it was working quite well if you asked me. Even if I had been helping, my father would have just pointed out the mistakes I made.

"Look, I should go. You are all better off without my presence," I said as I rose from my chair.

"Caleb, sit yourself down and finish what's on your plate. Girls! Hush now."

I sat down. My unease was now rapidly climbing, as the time to resolve my debt before my father came back, before the two-week deadline was waning.

"Tell me, " my mother interjected. Her voice was even, though I could already sense the weight of expectation behind it. "Have you heard anything about your father's ship?"

It had been weeks since his expected return. Everyone except for me was anxious for his arrival, my debt now hanging over me.

"Nothing yet."

"What are your plans for today? Straight to the tavern again, I suppose?" Alice said, smirking.

"That's enough," my mother snapped, her stare pausing on one sibling to the next. "Your father will be home any day now, and I've no interest in reporting mischief after his months at sea."

"Precisely," I agreed hastily.

"That is especially for you, Caleb Thompson," my mother said, her stern and dignified look reminding me of what was in store if she found out about my debt. "At twenty years, of all your siblings, you should have shown yourself the most orderly by now."

I took my last swallow of mush, got up, and left before I found myself in a more precarious position. I stepped out into the cool morning air, the door creaking behind me. That afternoon I went from one counting-house to the next, intent on securing a loan that might wipe the slate clean with Mr. Bellamy and spare my father the news of my recklessness. Yet every reputable lender declined me credit, while the less reputable paid me no respect. I considered liquidating the small library my father had so earnestly acquired for me. Those volumes would fetch a fair price, but their absence would certainly be noticed. The same dilemma arose: confession or a beating. The only thing saving me now was that I still had some time to figure it all out between the deadline I had and my father's return.

Chapter 3 (May) –
An Unjust Conscription

The following days were spent avoiding the tavern, dodging being tasked with unwanted duties related to the family business, and worrying how my father would respond to my gambling mess. From time to time, I paid Long Wharf a visit to see if there was any news of his return, hoping he was still delayed.

But on the third day I paid the wharf a visit, something happened that I will never forget. Long Wharf was a typical sight to see, with its weathered planks stretching long into the Boston Harbor, a bridge between land and the restless sea. Not long ago, its docks languished, collateral damage from the Revolutionary War, economic turmoil, and embargoes. But Boston's spirit was too stubborn to vanquish. Now, almost twenty years after the war, commerce was thriving once more, with the ceaseless rhythm of ships arriving and departing, of goods exchanged and fortunes made or sometimes lost. The breezy ocean air carried mingled scents of salt, fish, and exotic spices, the aroma of a town held together by trade. Tea, silk, and porcelain from the East. Sugar and cacao from the Caribbean. Lumber and flour bound for markets abroad. Goods spilled forth from the bellies of vessels, while shipwrights crouched at battered hulls, their calloused hands mending the wounds of months at sea. Where the harbor's edge met the docks, families gathered in small, hopeful clusters, their eyes scanning the decks of arriving ships, searching for familiar figures among the crowds of returning sailors and passengers. Warehouses and shops stretched and stood like sentinels along the pier, their facades worn by salt and time. On the docks, men moved with brisk efficiency, hauling crates and barrels from ships stationed in wharfage slips. Ships arrived from and bound to the West Indies, China, Europe, and beyond. If you had asked me, it was all too connected, too much obligation, too much pretense, too much political scheming.

I walked the length of the pier toward *Liberty*, which had just entered port, bound from the West Indies.

"Have you happened to have seen my father's ship?" I called out to the boatswain, Fletcher, whom I knew.

"Young Thompson! We have! Indeed, we have! I know her rigging. We spotted his ship just off the harbor, about a few miles behind us."

My heart began to pound rapidly. There was no more hiding my debt now. I waited for almost an hour, until a familiar shape emerged from the Outer Harbor. As the vessel drew nearer, I made out two square-rigged masts and sails full with the ocean breeze, propelling her swiftly towards the wharf. There was no mistaking the ship. It was certainly my father's heading toward me as though it knew I had a secret to confess.

Dodging crates and dockworkers, I raced down the wooden planks where there was an empty slip and waited, anxiously catching my breath. My mind raced. What could I possibly say to get out of the mess I was in? Shortly after I had caught my breath, Jameson, who had been performing carpentry work on a nearby ship, joined me.

When *Providence* came to rest, her crew swiftly disembarked. The sailors' faces were tight with urgency, their voices speaking in hushed tones, one to another. I scanned the deck for my father but could not spot him just yet. One by one, the crew stepped ashore, followed at last by the ship's first mate, Liam. His usual upright posture was crushed by something far worse than mere exhaustion from a long voyage.

"Boys!" he called, his voice carrying through the clamor. "Your father…"

"What? What happened?" I asked, feeling a rush of frantic energy throughout my body.

"The Royal Navy has taken your father!"

The words struck like a blow to my stomach. My breath hitched; my vision tunneled, the noise of the harbor a dull roar in my ears.

"Wait…what? What?" I managed, my throat tightening.

Liam hurried towards me, grabbed my shoulders, and looked me straight in the eyes.

"The Royal Navy," he said. "They conscripted your father!"

A mixture of shock and outrage rippled through those who stood by.

"Those damned scoundrels!" a sailor spat, his fists clenching. "They have no sense of honor!"

"This is why we need another war with them," another muttered darkly.

I clenched my jaw and shook my head in disbelief.

"I need to report this to the customs office. Let your mother know," Liam said, heading towards the customs house.

By the time Jameson and I arrived home, my breath came in ragged bursts, the news of my father's conscription still shocking to my soul. I rushed through the front door, through the kitchen past my sisters and through the hall until I reached the parlor where my mother sat reading. Jameson, following in just after.

"Father has been conscripted!" I called out, the words shaky as they left my mouth.

Startled, her hands faltered on the book she held. "What?!" mother's voice broke.

"The Royal Navy took him," I said, looking at her.

She dropped her book, sitting in silence.

"*Providence* just arrived back without Father."

"I know, I heard you. I just don't believe it…Are you sure? What did Liam say?" she asked, trying to make sense of it all.

"He said he was reporting the incident to the customs office."

"I don't understand," she said, her voice cracking. "Why would they take him?"

I shook my head, unable to answer. The uncertainty of what the future held made my mind numb. The room seemed to fold in on itself. Jameson stood still and slowly began to crouch into a chair. My sisters, who had entered the room, began to cry, sobbing in desperation. Mother got up to console them, pulling them close.

"I am sure this will work out. After the report from the customs office is reported up the chain of command," I said with confidence, yet deep inside, I doubted my words.

My mother continued to hold my sisters tight, her face full of uncertainty.

"I hope you are right."

"Mother, what are we to do?" Charlotte said, wiping her eyes.

"We all shall do our part and stand by one another until his return."

Her words weighed heavily. Now more than ever, I needed my father back.

"Do you truly think he'll return?" Alice said, still sobbing.

"Of course," Mother replied. "Hear me now. I want all of you beside me in church come Sunday," she said, straightening her back as she held in her pain.

The room fell silent, each of us turning inward, measuring the significance of Alice's question.

Chapter 4 (May) – Beneath the Surface

With my father gone, the future of the family business was uncertain. Though my mother was competent to take over the business, between the domestic responsibilities, the management of accounts, coordinating the shipments, and keeping the ledgers in order, it was simply too much for one person to manage efficiently. That left me with a fearful burden of entanglements and responsibilities I'd not volunteered for. Yet my mother, as full of faith as anyone, insisted I start helping by untangling the family ledger.

"Caleb, I need you to go down to your father's counting room and set the books in order."

For a moment, I held a blank stare, trying to understand her words. "I don't know that I'm the one you ought to be asking."

"I know full well what's passed between you and your father, but now is the time to set that aside. Go down, have a look, and see what you find."

My mind flooded with excuses to get out of her request. But I could tell she was urging me on. I knew it didn't make sense to argue with her. At least not now, with her faith clearly in me, though I couldn't see why.

"I will take a look. But don't get it in your mind that I am committing to this. I…"

"I know well enough what you would say," she interposed. "You have my consent. The responsibility rests with you now, as before."

I reluctantly nodded, frustrated by the request, and headed towards the wharf.

As I made my way towards the storehouses along the wharf, where the family counting room stood, the large debt I was in followed me in my burdened mind. I entered the large storehouse building containing warehouses on the first floor and counting rooms on the second, mulling over my limited options. I climbed the stairs when I reached the family counting room. Above the office door, the wooden sign of the Atlantic Shipping Co. hung, its bold lettering framed a painted ship cleaving through stormy seas. My heart raced as though I too was in a perilous situation as my father.

When I entered the counting room, I began to feel the burden and enormity of what had taken place over the course of the past few days. Reminders of him were everywhere. From the telescope he had on his desk that I gravitated to as a young boy, to the stern silhouette portrait of him on the wall, to the row of neatly trimmed quills and the tall, high-backed chair he occupied for countless hours into the candlelit night. Every detail spoke of his disciplined rigor. Heavy ledgers and piles of parchment lay stacked on his broad oak desk, columns of numbers tracking every shipment, payment, and outstanding balance. I once knew these ledgers well, and for unfortunate reasons, they haunted me.

As I stood at the desk near the window, the immediacy of my trouble continued to wane on me. Before I could delve deeper into the health of the business, I had to think fast about how to pay Mr. Bellamy back. Gambling more was an option I quickly dismissed. I dared not to enter the basement of the Green Dragon Tavern again with John lurking there. The faint scent of ink and parchment hung in the air as I sat at my father's wooden desk. I flipped through the neatly inked pages, searching for a balance owed I could possibly collect on or inventory I could sell. Then, if I could simply borrow the money from the transaction, I could eventually pay it back without being detected. Staring at the endless entries, I began to fall into a trance, retracing how my father even had arrived at this point.

My father, along with the rest of the Thompson family, arrived in Boston in the wake of the war, settling into a town where the embers of revolution still glowed beneath the surface. With a single-masted sloop named *Friendship*, he ventured into the uncertain waters of trade, carrying rum, timber, and textiles to the West Indies in exchange for molasses, sugar, and exotic spices. It was a game of patience and peril, each voyage a gamble against storms, disease, and the unpredictable nature of bad actors on the open sea. As his fortunes grew, so too did his fleet. He acquired *Eleanor*, a sleek schooner built for speed and cargo, deepening our ties to the West Indies trade. With her, we shipped flour, finished goods, and salted meats, returning with commodities that kept Boston's economy churning and its harbor alive with commerce: even more sugar, molasses, and barrels of coffee. But it was

Providence, our third and most prized vessel, that stood as the pinnacle of his endeavors. A brig built for endurance, she carried heavier cargo to the farthest reaches of the Caribbean hauling flour, salted fish, and livestock. Returning with coffee, spices, and fruits that merchants in Boston seized eagerly. The Atlantic Shipping Co. began as a humble endeavor but had since carved out its own respectable success. Where others saw risk, my father saw opportunity. And now, with Napoleon's war tightening its grip across Europe and the seas, the challenges had only multiplied.

As I opened the ledger, searching for an entry that could benefit me, I paused. Here I was, scheming to find my way out of a debt, while my family stood on the brink of tragedy and my father facing peril far away. Though the harbor was brimming, I was empty inside. I felt so utterly alone, as though I had been set adrift beyond the harbor's reach, lost upon the vast blue sea. I took a long breath, then began scanning the ledgers as memories of my father showing me how to read the entries flooded my mind. I thought if there was any place to start, it was when he departed on his last voyage. I flipped to an entry dated the week before his ship left port:

February 7th, 1805

Partial payment of forty ounces of silver with remaining amount of three hundred forty five ounces of silver to be settled in full in exchange for one thousand pounds of Indigo. Pick up location, St. Kitts.

Who pays that much up front? And why would he venture out that far? I thought as I leaned in, furrowing my brow. Questions remained as I turned toward the mahogany shelves where my father kept the business contracts. I thumbed through the pile until I found the contract tied to the transaction I had just studied.

Spreading the contract across the desk, I scanned the lines of neatly written text.

"New England Mercantile Co.," I read aloud.

I flipped the contract over, then back over again, but found no address. What I did find was precarious: "Customer pickup at the warehouse by Mr. Prescott." I had never heard of this company. I wondered if they were from New Hampshire or Connecticut, or possibly Rhode Island, and that was the reason they were obscure.

I stepped outside, but the air felt different. As I walked along the docks of Long Wharf, the weight of my father's absence hung heavy on my shoulders. Ahead, the ships of the harbor loomed beneath gathering clouds beginning to block the sun. Indifferent to my troubles, the activities of the harbor continued while the shadow of British power reminded me of the many dangers of international waters. When I arrived at *Providence*, still being emptied of its cargo, I found Liam.

Liam's shoulders were still slumped, the haunting of my father's conscription hanging over him like a dark cloud. I climbed the gangway onto the deck.

"Caleb, good to see you son. Did you inform your mother of your father's plight?

"Yes, I did, yesterday."

"I won't lie. I don't know if I will ever shake this burden. I informed the customs officer of your father's conscription."

"What did they say?"

"They mean to report the matter straightaway to President Jefferson. The customs officer assured me that such cases are treated with all seriousness. Yet, truth be told, I cannot say how swiftly they might move without the hand of the military."

The thought of my father not coming back soon filled my belly with dread. "Can I see the shipping manifest?"

"Of course, it's still on the ship."

Liam hailed the second mate. "Fetch me the manifest, will ya?"

As the sailor departed, I headed into the captain's quarters, while Liam stood outside the door. The room still bore the imprint of my father with the faint scent of pipe smoke lingering in the air. Documents and nautical instruments were scattered across his desk. I walked to the desk and shuffled through the documents when I found a map with a carefully planned route laid out in full detail. I followed each marker on the map, from home port to each landfall, then to what appeared to be the final stop.

"Is this where the conscription happened?" I asked, pointing to a spot near St. Kitts.

Liam entered slowly and glanced at where I was pointing. "Right. That's where those lobsterbacks took your father!"

Moments later, we heard knocking on the door.

"Come in!" Liam shouted.

The second mate opened the door and stood with the manifest in hand, hesitant to enter. Liam looked at me, then walked over to him.

"Here it is," the second mate said, passing the manifest to Liam. "Do you think you should be in there?" he whispered.

"Just go," Liam replied.

Liam approached and said, "He is every bit in the same mind frame as I," as he placed the manifest on the desk.

My hands trembled as I unfolded it. I scanned the document, each entry listed goods and destinations, until I spotted the transaction tied to the indigo entry from the ledger.

"This shipment of indigo is odd."

"The goods were procured at St. Kitts."

"I don't understand why he would go that far out of the normal way," I asked, shaking my head.

"Just before we departed, he signed the contract," Liam said, pausing before continuing. "He said it was a chance to expand business. The crew was for it. In the end, as odd as the timing was, it appeared like a good prospect."

The words, "a good prospect," sat uneasily. I still did not fully understand why he ventured out so far out of his normal route. "This is not adding up."

"No, it doesn't."

"How did the Royal Navy end up boarding the ship?"

"A Man-O-War began to follow us when we departed port from St. Kitts. Your father ordered us to sail on as the Man-O-War approached. We continued for a while but could not outrun it. When the ship got close enough, they fired cannon, which as customary would have been a warning. But it struck the side of the ship and caused damage," Liam said, his voice low. "After they fired at us, he told the men to heave to and anchor. That's when the Royal Navy boarded. The men were stunned. This wasn't something any of us had faced before. Other plights, but not the

British firing at us from a Man-O-War carrying 100 guns! The strangest thing is… I'll never forget it…they went straight for your father!"

Liam tilted his head downwards, raising his hand to his forehead. He raised his head, looked at me and took a deep breath. "Then they brought him out starboard and signaled to their captain, calling out his name. Captain Rotheram, his name was, that beast. He shouted back to the men holding your father, 'That is our man!' And just like that, they took him off the ship… I still don't believe it happened."

What Liam shared left me pondering. "I don't believe it either," I said looking down at the planks. After a brief pause, I asked, "It looks like they were looking for something in here?"

"While navymen held us back, a few officers came in here," Liam said. He fixed a fierce yet sincere gaze at me. "The men were ready to fight, but your father instructed us to stand down."

I nodded, knowing full well he meant what he said. "What do you think they were looking for?" I asked, scanning the room.

"His journal, most likely. They rummaged through everything," Liam said, his eyes narrowing.

"Why would they want his journal?"

"To cover their tracks, I suppose. I am sure he was detailing everything up until the point they boarded."

I observed the wooden desk. Its drawers were pulled open, the contents scattered haphazardly: quills, charts, and a half-empty bottle of ink. My hands ran along the underside of the desk until I found the hidden compartment. I first discovered it when I was a boy, while my father planned a route. He had kept his money and maps there when he traveled upon the seas. My heart quickened as I opened the compartment, and there was his captain's journal, untouched. I pulled it free, clutching it as if it were fragile. I opened it slowly. The worn leather cover faintly crackled, the pages filled with his precise handwriting. I skimmed entries, my eyes catching several towards the last few pages:

April 7th, 1805

The men have noticed a Man-O-War following us. They are growing uneasy.

April 8th, 1805

There is unrest among the crew. They've begun to question our voyage to St. Kitts. I assured them all is well, but their unease lingers.

April 10th, 1805

The first transaction with Indigo has been completed successfully. Yet, the Man-O-War that had been shadowing us remains offshore. Some men are warning me not to depart until it leaves. Others are demanding we depart in another direction.

April 13th, 1805

The men's suspicions were well-founded. The Man-O-War anchored offshore is now in pursuit.

April 16th, 1805

The HMS Royal Sovereign has fired upon us, causing some damage in the starboard. We have not caused provocation. I ordered my men to stand down and anchor.

My stomach tightened as I read the final entry. My fear magnified as I worried about the danger he was in. The actions of the Royal Navy seemed as though they were hunting him down, rather than trying to find bodies to man their ships. Hoping to find any sense in it all, I flipped back to earlier pages. I stopped on an entry detailing his departure:

February 15th, 1805

We have just left the harbor, bound for the West Indies. This time, our route ends at St. Kitts. This was an unusual choice brought about by an opportunity so great it could transform the family business for years to come. The men are thrilled. This is not just trade, but the chance to elevate our standing, to escape the mundane and seize something greater. Still, I find the arrangement peculiar, and some doubts stir within me. Too sudden, too tied to a man I had never met before. He went by the last name Presctott. Though he was wealthy, that much was clear. A middle-aged man, perhaps in his late forties, a wig, dressed impeccably, his fine coat and the br— red—, that he noticeably kept fidgeting. On it was what appeared to be a f—n.

The entry was incomplete, and beyond recognition with the final description smudged before the ink had dried. I ran my finger over the ink, trying to decipher it. But that did not help.

"Red what?" I muttered, leaning closer. The words remained stubbornly illegible, a small yet maddening detail.

"What is it?" Liam asked.

"I don't know yet. If this was a coincidence, it was an awfully precise one," I said. "Have you heard of the last name Prescott?"

"It doesn't sound familiar, no. Why do you ask?"

"That's the name on the contract for the indigo shipment. This deal, the British ship, the conscription. It all feels eerily connected.

But maybe I am wrong. We'll have to wait until the goods are picked up to gather more information."

"I suppose so… I forgot… Did we depart on a Friday?" Liam asked.

"Your superstitions are growing, aren't they?"

"I am sorry, Caleb. I just want to be able to understand this all. Perhaps if I'd done something different, this could have been avoided."

"It's not your fault," I replied, looking at Liam. The shame in his eyes revealed a burden of guilt I wasn't sure he would ever recover from.

"I'll stay here and unload the cargo. Do let me know if you need anything."

I nodded then exited the disheveled quarters, now only a semblance of my father's presence.

Before I stepped onto the gangway, Liam stopped me. "Caleb…by the way, John Lowe was around here earlier this morning asking about your father. He was being quite forceful in his questioning… Any reason he might be looking for him?"

"Not a clue," I replied, though I knew very well why he was coming around.

I walked in silence, my anxieties beginning to swell. The Royal Navy had taken my father, yet there were more questions than answers now. What was becoming clearer was that he was in danger, maybe more so than I knew. And no one was coming to save him soon. Or me.

Returning home, I found my mother in the cool cellar, gathering roots and vegetables for dinner. With the doors open wide, I descended the steps to her side.

"Caleb! I almost finished," she replied, her hands still at task.

While I stood there, I glanced over at the corner of the room where my father's chest was. My mother took notice.

"I can meet you up in the kitchen once I am done," she said, hurrying to get everything in the basket as quickly as possible.

"I need to tell you what I found," I said, my heart beginning to pump fast.

"Can't it wait?"

"Well, no. I found a strange transaction in Father's ledger. An entry tied to where the conscription took place."

"What do you mean? Wait… The St. Kitts transaction?" she inquired as she grabbed the full basket, ushering me back towards the entrance.

"Yes, that one. What do you know about it?"

"Your father told me about the contract he signed before he left. He said it was the start of a new promising account."

"Do you know who Mr. Prescott is?"

"I don't," she replied as we continued up the stairs and out of the frigid cellar.

"Well, he paid upfront in a significant amount of silver. That is risky if you ask me."

I closed the doors to the cellar while my mother stood by, wondering if she was thinking the same way I was.

"Maybe? He probably was solidifying the deal if you ask me."

I paused as she stood with the basket close to her body, wanting to continue towards the front door.

"Possibly. But then, the way Liam described his conscription, it's as though they were looking for him specifically."

"Let's go, this is heavy." she said as she began heading back towards the front door.

"Here, give me the basket."

"Let us go in. I've dinner to begin," she insisted. Turning to me with a searching look, she added, "Are you telling me this trade is connected to your father's conscription?"

I opened the door and we entered.

"I am not saying that exactly. Well…I suppose I am. It's just odd that he went out that far, then was conscripted by the Royal Navy, who seemed to single him out. They also tried to find his journal. But he hid it."

"How do you know?" My mother stopped as she placed the basket on the table.

"I found it!" I said, holding the journal up.

"Let me see it," she said, extending her hand.

I reluctantly handed it over. I wanted to consume its contents more, yet by giving it over, I hoped I could have another chance. My mother held it in her hands, skimming it. Then she placed it onto the table.

"Can I have it back?"

"Let's talk about this more some other time," she said, handing the journal to me. "How will things look over the course of the next few weeks?"

"I didn't get that far," I admitted. "Once I found this transaction, I went to ask Liam about it. But I'll head back this week."

She gave me a brisk nod. "Good."

My sisters, who had just joined the kitchen, hung a large kettle over the fire in the hearth. I stepped out of the kitchen and stood in the doorway.

"I'll leave you to it," I said quietly. She didn't look my way. "Yes. Another time. But don't forget, we need to stay focused on what keeps things running."

I turned away and headed up toward my room. Part of me wondered if I was imagining things, if possibly, I was being emotional or irrational. But I couldn't shake the notion that there was more to find out. That the truth was somewhere near, though elusive.

Chapter 5 (June) –
A Gaze at The Old North Church

By the time Sunday morning came, my family, ever dutiful in ritual and reputation, set out for Old North Church. I went along, not out of an expression of faith, but because if there was any place where I could gather more information about the New England Mercantile Co., it was at the church. Its narrow, towering brick façade was a mottled tapestry of deep reds and russets, spotted here and there with darker patches where years of dampness had settled in. The steeple, marred by a gale, had once crowned the church as if to remind Boston of its lore: the lantern signal, the midnight ride, the revolution that followed. Yet now it lay bare, as though its past had been forgotten.

As we passed through the large wooden doors, the interior was unexpectedly bright, with soaring ceilings, astonishing in their grandeur. A large brass chandelier hung from a stout chain, gleaming in the morning light. Box pews were lined in rows, straight and square. Each one was scuffed and softened from decades of families pressing against the rails. Inside each pew were family prayer books neatly tucked into shelves. Along both sides, tall windows cast long beams of light across the floorboards. For all its beauty, the building held a kind of majesty that made me keenly aware of the unspoken sins resting on my chest.

Here, on the first floor, conversations carried on between men and women who fancied themselves veterans of the sea, of commerce, of the delicate dance between opportunity and ruin. People clustered in small, predictable groups, their discussion shifting between the usual town tidbits, cargo prices, the latest on the Napoleonic War, and the ever-looming specter of America getting dragged into another war with Britain. It was less a conversation and more of a performance that they seemed content to repeat every Sunday.

Above, in the unpaid pews, sat freedmen and freedwomen, apprentices, sailors between voyages, and the town's working class. Their hands, roughened by labor; their clothes, simpler; yet their presence no less reverent, rather with a similar aim to show that they too were devoted. Why someone would, week after week, have bound themselves to such routine obligation, I could not comprehend.

I lingered with my family, half-listening to the blend of commercial speculation and political discourse. My attention focused on ways to make a connection with someone who might know something about the New England Mercantile Company. That was when the opportunity I was looking for came walking our way as we were greeted by Capt. Malcolm, one of the more prominent ship owners in Boston.

"I want you to know I fully support your family during this difficult time," he said while removing his tricorn hat. His tone carried the assurance of a man whose words beheld credibility. "I trust Mr. Thompson will return and that you will overcome this misfortune."

"Thank you. You know Charlotte, Alice, Jameson, and Caleb," my mother said, motioning towards us.

I straightened, acknowledging him with a nod. If anyone would have known about the various businesses in town, it was him.

"I do hope the Atlantic Shipping Co. will endure in his absence," Capt. Malcolm said, looking at my mother.

My mother's smile was pleasant, but her voice was firm. "Yes, of course. Operations will continue as usual."

"Very good," he replied, his expression unreadable. "If there is any assistance I can provide, please do let me know."

By assistance, I knew he did not mean charity. He meant assets sold, ships offloaded, or worse, the company itself relinquished into his hands. My mother and the captain continued to discuss the affairs of the family business, so much so that I could not get a single word in.

I let my gaze drift over the entering crowd, when I noticed a young woman stepping into the church amid a wave of townspeople. The flickering light from the high-set windows caught her brilliant red hair that was half-pinned, the front drawn back into a modest knot, leaving the remainder free in soft waves. Her green eyes met mine with quiet curiosity. For a moment, the voices around me dulled, their words blurring into meaningless static. I retraced my memory, trying to recall the last time I had set foot in Old North, let alone whether I had ever seen her before.

Behind her, familiar faces emerged, Mr. and Mrs. Hayes. As the owner of the Standard Shipping Co., Mr. Hayes carried himself with the ease of a man accustomed to having command. His chiseled jawline, large amber eyes, and a mane of dark brown hair streaked with silver spoke to a natural charm cultivated by the sharp discipline of a man who had seen success and difficulties yet came out stronger for it. His clothing was impeccable: a perfectly uniform tricorn hat; a light gray frock coat; his breeches, tailored to no fault, tucked neatly into polished leather boots.

Beside him stood Mrs. Hayes, a portrait of flawless refinement. Her porcelain skin; her raven-colored hair, intricately styled; and her gown, a deep, sumptuous brocade. She moved with the practiced mannerisms of a woman accustomed to admiration, every tilt of her chin, every measured step, as carefully curated as a fine portrait framed in gold. She greeted friends with polite pleasantries, the corners of her mouth lifting just enough to suggest warmth, but not enough to promise sincerity.

While Mrs. Hayes mingled with her friends, Mr. Hayes fell into conversation with a younger-looking man, clad in a black frock coat and breeches. Their exchange struck me as decidedly businesslike. After a firm handshake, the man quietly slipped out of the church, seemingly unconcerned with the sermon.

The young woman I assumed was their daughter moved through the crowd, greeted by smiling faces, her demeanor warm. She had inherited her parents' looks, that much was certain, but something about her was different. Where her mother's charm was calculated, hers seemed natural. Where her father's presence commanded respect, hers welcomed it. There was an ease to her, as if she carried herself without the weight of expectation, or at least, without letting it show.

My attention had been so focused on the young woman I failed to realize Capt. Malcom was already heading away. The congregation proceeded to fill the seats with the quiet purpose of ritual. My mother led my siblings to our pew: a paid seat among the city's captains, merchants, and men of trade. But I couldn't let my chance go, to inquire about the New England Mercantile Co.

I caught up to Capt. Malcolm and called out amidst the quieting crowd. "Excuse me, Captain!"

He turned around, his face filled with riddles.

I found myself torn in two directions. If what I was about to ask was baseless, I'd come off as a lunatic. But if he knew something, he might help me find the answers I needed.

"Would you happen to know of a company called the New England Mercantile Co.?"

A brief, almost blank glance passed upon his eyes before he replied, "Never heard of them. Why do you ask?"

I hesitated. "Just...something I came across. It isn't very important."

Capt. Malcolm studied me, his gaze lingering just a moment too long. I forced a casual nod, but my pulse quickened. *Did I just make a mistake?*

"If they were reputable, I would have heard of them," he replied.

"Do you know the name Mr. Prescott?"

"I have no knowledge of that name," he replied, standing there half turned, ready to depart my presence. "Is that all?"

"That is all, thank you. Good day," I replied awkwardly, my eyes shifting towards the floor.

He departed to his pew and so to mine, leaving me with no additional answers than before. The hum of conversation turned to slight whispers as Reverend Asa Eaton ascended to the pulpit. His black robe billowed slightly with each step. Sunlight was beaming on the pulpit square in the center, bathing it in a pale glow. Behind the pulpit stood a great Palladian window, its three parts stretching from floor to ceiling. The white bands hanging at his neck framed a solemn face, one etched with experience, wisdom, and the quiet authority of a man who had long ago mastered the art of holding a congregation in rapt attention. Yet I could not sit still as uncomfortable silence settled over the room.

"Welcome, brothers and sisters," Reverend Eaton began, his voice carrying through the rafters.

"Before we commence worship, we must address a matter of great concern. As many of you have come to know, Mr. Thompson has been recently conscripted into the Royal Navy. A pillar of our community, a man of good character, he is in need of our prayers. Let us appeal to our Heavenly Father for his safe return."

The congregation bowed their heads in unison. The reverend's words landed heavily, sorrow aching in my chest. My father's absence had been a fact before, but now, spoken aloud before so many witnesses, it became a reality impossible to ignore. In a way, it made me more agitated since I could do nothing but listen.

When the prayer ended, my mother lifted her gaze, scanning the congregation with her customary grace. "We are deeply appreciative of your support," she said, her voice smooth, unyielding.

The reverend continued, "My friends, you are all mindful that the steeple of this house of worship has forever been a sign to our town and our nation…the place from which the signal was given in our hour of peril, whether the enemy advanced by land or by sea. Today, we give humble thanks for the benevolence of Mr. and Mrs. Hayes, whose gift shall make it possible to restore the steeple. May their kindness be a light unto us, as the steeple itself shall once more be a light to this community."

Mr. and Mrs. Hayes nodded in acknowledgment, their expressions composed. Beside them, the young woman lowered her head modestly. With that, the sermon began, and I was reminded, once again, why I did not make a habit of attending service.

"Throughout life, we often wrestle with the conflict between where our faithfulness should stay true," the reverend intoned, his cadence measured, deliberate. "Now this may sound controversial, but above all things, we should pursue loyalty to sound virtues. And in this, if we all have this same individual pursuit, we collectively have a functioning society."

I tried to focus, but my attention faltered. My gaze shifted from the pulpit to the Hayes' pew where the young girl sat and back again. My thoughts broke apart, fragmented. A part of the sermon here, a fleeting glance there, and beneath it all, the steady reminder of my father's absence, pressing deeper by the moment. The service carried on, the cadence of it predictable and unchanging: prayers, scripture, hymns.

When the service ended, the congregation rose to their feet, their thoughts transitioning from piety back to business, busy-talk, and politics. My mother stood among her friends, speaking with dignified ease, no doubt recounting my father's conscription, the family's resilience, the steadfast nature of the family business. I lingered, feeling uneasy, displaced, as though I had stepped into someone else's life, playing a role I had not yet learned the lines for. Across the room, the Hayes family made their departure with measured steps.

Not soon enough, we departed as well. As we stepped outside, the fervor of the morning service still clung to the townspeople spilling out into the streets paved with cobblestones. My family seemed comforted by the outpouring of support of the community. I, however, felt none of it. My thoughts swirled with anxiety as the streets began to swarm with people, carriages, and people pulling carts. Perhaps my nervousness was from the pressure of having to repay Mr. Bellamy before my time ran out. Perhaps it was the uncertainty surrounding my father's fate, the helplessness of waiting for answers that seemed as though they may never arrive. Or perhaps it was something more, something I hadn't yet placed my finger on.

My family headed back home while I went in a different direction towards the market. I recalled that there was a busy dressmaker near Dock Square who sold clothing with various dyes, including indigo, so I paid the shop a visit.

When I entered the dressmaker's shop, the scent of linen and beeswax filled the air. There were rolled-up fabrics of various colors and materials stacked in rows to the right. Ribbons, laces, pins, and other materials lay in cubbyholes beneath a measuring table. Near the wall on the left, a young woman stood tall before a mirror. Her mother inspected the gown she wore, tugging the sleeves gently. The seamstress, with her sleeves rolled up and a measuring tape looped around her neck, was busy marking fabric at a long wooden counter.

"How can I help you, young man?" the seamstress asked.

"Is the owner present today?"

"That would be me. How can I help you?"

"Well, I have an odd question of sorts. We had recently brought back a shipment of indigo, and I would like to know more about your sources of materials."

"Oh. Yes. We have a contract with someone already. We are not looking to separate from the existing relationship we have."

The seamstress peered over my shoulders.

"Do you like the gown? Does it fit well?"

"Yes, I love it," the young woman replied.

"I can take payment and provide a receipt if you would like."

"That would be fantastic," the mother said.

"Give me one moment, please."

I stood off the side while the seamstress collected payment, then went to the back. The young woman and her mother walked back to the mirror to bask in the beauty of the newly fitted gown. While I stood there, I noticed the order-book on the counter, its pages wide open. I drifted back to the counter, keeping an eye on the others in the room. I slowly turned the book around and began to read the entries:

Apr 5th, 1805 – Miss A. Boylston
Morning gown in pale lawn, lace collar, narrow sleeve. Due: May 18th.

Apr 8th, 1805 – Mrs. Bradlee (for niece)
Walking dress, striped. Lined bodice, short puff sleeve, no trim. Required for Sunday.

…

Apr 12th, 1805 – Mrs. R. Langdon
Widow's dress, black wool. Plain cuffs, no ornament. Full mourning. Due: May 3.

My body shook when the owner called out, "I will be right there, I am just entering the transaction into the ledger."

"No rush!" the mother replied.

I stood still. Then, when I knew I wasn't being observed, I continued to slowly flip each page, scanning the names of older entries when I stopped on a page. The top of the entry read:

March 2nd, 1805 – Miss Maryann Hayes

One walking dress, indigo-dyed muslin, high waist, fitted back, gathered skirt. Short sleeve, modest neckline, unlined.

When I read the last entry I realized that Maryann must be the name of the young woman I saw at church.

As I attempted to read further, I heard the owner shuffling back towards the counter. But before I could turn the order-book around, the mother and daughter had already come back towards the counter and stood next to me. I moved over, hoping the owner would not notice my intrusion. The owner handed over a receipt.

"All work is guaranteed."

"We don't plan on returning this one. You did a fine job. Thank you."

The mother and daughter left the shop and went their merry way. To distract the owner from noticing anything out of place, I caught her attention.

"If you will, back to my inquiry. I was not so much trying to solicit business but curious if you had ever heard of the New England Mercantile Co.?"

She paused, her mouth clinched, her brows folded. She shook her head. "Never heard of them."

"Hmm…well, then, sorry to bother you. I will be on my way."

I left in an uncomfortable hurry, before the owner found her order book had been combed through. The more I considered the New England Mercantile Co., the stranger it seemed. Capt. Malcolm was well-connected. If he had never heard of the company, what did that mean? Even still, the more prominent dressmaker who sourced indigo to dye clothing never heard of the company either. My mother or father did not know him either. It was clear that I had come to an impasse, and that brought me great consternation.

Chapter 6 (June) – Fateful Introductions

When morning broke, I rose quickly with a jolt of nervous energy pulsing me rapidly awake. I made my way downstairs and into the parlor where the family bookcase stood. Our family had acquired numerous books for study and entertainment over time. Some belonged to me, acquired by my father to encourage me to read. I stacked the books that belonged to me into a crate. I counted all nineteen, from *The Death of Captain Cook* to the encyclopedia set I owned. Each title, a past indulgence. Each spine, a memory. I heard footsteps approaching; then Charlotte appeared at the threshold.

"What are you doing with your books?" she asked, watching me carefully.

"Going to sell them," I replied, forcing my voice into casual indifference.

She came closer and looked at me with a frown. She plucked *The Death of Captain Cook* from the top of the pile. "But this one's your favorite… Father bought these for you."

"I don't have a choice."

"What do you mean? Those are worth far more than any price someone might pay!"

I didn't linger. I couldn't. Gathering the books, I slipped from the house and set off toward Thomas & Andrews, the town's most reputable bookseller. The wooden door creaked as I entered, struggling to hold the crate full of books.

From the back office, the shopkeeper's voice rang out. "Just a moment. I'll be right with you."

I set the crate down on the counter, exhaling, before letting my eyes wander. The shop was a maze of countless tales and histories, its shelves crammed with volumes old and new. My fingers drifted over book spines before settling on a familiar title, *Arthur Mervyn,* a story about a young man who was faced with formidable challenges by Charles Brockden Brown. I flipped through its pages absently, the rustling paper stirring a quiet unease. I had once devoured books, letting them carry me to far-off places. But at one point in time, that changed. And I couldn't recall when I had stopped or why.

While I stood holding the book, the bells at the shop door jingled. I glanced up and found myself caught completely off guard. There she was. The young woman from church. She stepped inside with her effortless grace, her gown a shade of deep blue, its rich fabric catching the light, framing her red hair in a way that made it seem almost aflame. Up close, she was even more striking. Her skin was fair and impeccable, and her eyes were deep and full as an untamed forest. My heart hammered with a reckless thrill eerily like the rush I got from gambling. Her presence was calming and unnerving, like the still air before a storm.

"Hello… Miss Hayes, is it?" I greeted her in haste, attempting to keep my voice steady.

She paused and gave me the most curious expression. "Have we met?"

I cleared my throat. "I know of your parents. Mr. and Mrs. Hayes, am I right? The pastor mentioned your family's generous donation this Sunday at church."

Her face lit up. "Oh, right! I am sorry, you just seemed familiar, and I didn't recall where we might have met. Call me Maryann." She looked at me as though reading through her memory, then said, "Mr. Thompson, correct?"

Hearing her say my last name sent a jolt of joy throughout my body.

"Yes, but you can call me Caleb. It's a pleasure to meet you."

Then, with a sincere tone, she said, "I'm so sorry to hear about your father."

And there it was. The reason she knew my name. Not because I had done anything remarkable nor from our paths ever crossing before. Rather, it was because my father had been ripped from his ship, his fate uncertain, his absence the talk of Boston.

Still, I managed to nod. "Thank you. That is kind of you."

Maryann's focus moved to the book in my hand. "Do you enjoy reading?"

Shame washed over me, extinguishing every last spark of excitement.

"I did at one point in time," I said, setting the book back in its place.

Before she could say more, the shopkeeper emerged, peering at my stack of books.

"Are you here to sell these, young man?"

I hesitated. Then, with a reluctant nod, I replied, "Unfortunately, yes."

Confusion and curiosity flickered across Maryann's face. I tried to focus on the shopkeeper, but I felt her eyes on me.

"Excuse me, Maryann," I said, walking back to the shopkeeper.

"Very fine encyclopedia set," he said, his eyes gleaming.

We bargained for a few moments before settling on an amount. I pocketed the shillings, the weight of them relieving. As I turned to leave, Maryann lingered at a shelf near the counter, her eyes tracing rows of books.

"It was very nice to meet you, Maryann," I said, preparing to leave.

She looked up, holding a book in her hands. "What do you think of this one?"

I glanced at the title, *The Mysteries of Udolpho.*

I smiled. "That is a fantastic read. I highly recommend it."

Her lips curved slightly, her fingers brushing the worn cover. "I've heard about it but never took the opportunity to read it."

"You should."

For a moment, I hesitated, searching for a reason to remain a bit longer.

Maryann seemed to sense it, offering me an escape before I embarrassed myself.

"Oh, by the way," she added lightly, "will you be at the Fourth of July celebration?"

In the past, my enthusiasm for the celebration was guided by the excuse for merriment. However, my father took the celebration seriously. He made it a point to participate when he was not out at sea. But no matter what, he always donated to the festivities. With him being gone, the event had yet to enter my thoughts.

"Yes, of course," I answered. "Our family always attends. My father donates toward the fireworks every year." The words felt hollow, given the circumstances.

Her eyes brightened. "Isn't it a splendid celebration? The spirit of the town comes alive."

"It is quite remarkable, given how far Boston has come after the war. The turmoil, the division…the siege. Now it feels like every port in the world connects back here. The West Indies, Europe, China," I replied, though deep down, all the bustle gave me severe unease.

She nodded. "Well put and makes perfect sense why the town is so alive on that day." Then, after a pause, "I hope and pray for your family. May you find strength and see your father safely return home."

I swallowed. Her warm words filled my soul with comfort. "Thank you. I hope to see you at the celebration."

I left the shop, but my mind remained in the bookstore. Maryann's beauty and kindness humbled me. She stood apart from the rest, genuinely considerate in a way many others were not. Yet the regard we shared dared me to believe I might be worthy of her.

Chapter 7 (June) – Settled Debts

While I walked toward Long Wharf to Mr. Bellamy's office, I anxiously anticipated what it would feel like when my debt was finally settled. The afternoon air of the harbor was scented with the tang of tar, salt, and cod. At the head of the wharf stood the port-watchman, with his lanky body and long arms adjusting a lantern to ensure it was straight. I quickly passed by him heading onto the thick and sturdy planks of the docks towards the countinghouses and storerooms. Each step toward Mr. Bellamy's office felt heavy as if I was walking toward judgment. I strolled past the windows of the office of Bellamy Trading Co. yet I did not notice any sign of activity inside. I came to the entrance, the company sign hanging to the side, but the door was locked.

I continued to walk along the docks, while the ocean water lapped against the wooden pilings covered in barnacles and green algae. Various-sized ships' masts spread out like a forest in the harbor. Barrels of rum were being lifted onto a nearby ship while the sound of construction clanged from India Wharf nearby. Farther ahead down the docks was the familiar bellow of John Lowe. His voice carried over the strained grunts of men hauling crates into the belly of waiting ships. I approached the ship he was on, aiming to get in and out as fast as possible. If I hadn't already been unnerved enough, the ship's ghastly carved figurehead—a three-headed dog depicting Cerberus, the hound of hades, with its glaring red eyes watched from the bow—reminded me just who I was dealing with.

I continued towards where John stood on the quarterdeck as he shouted out orders. His gaze swept the docks before landing on me. When he noticed me, his mouth curled into a wolfish grin.

"Caleb!" he shouted, spreading his arms wide in mock welcome. "You must be here to ask for more time, am I right?"

I forced my shoulders square and kept my voice even. "I'm here to see Mr. Bellamy."

His grin widened, slow and knowing. "You know he's busy," he shot back. "And you know if you want to talk to him, you can go through me."

I clenched my jaw. "I'd prefer to pay Mr. Bellamy myself. I have the money."

John leaned against the side of the ship, observing me how a predator would eye trapped prey. "What, you don't trust me to deliver the payment? Get up here then!" He gestured with a wave.

I climbed the wooden gangway plank leading onto the deck of the ship. Then, John led me to the quarterdeck, weaving and dodging sailors and barrels along the way. Everything in my body told me to turn back, but I kept forging on, my nerves trembling each step I made against the wooden planks.

"Tell me…how'd you get the money with your father not being around? Raid the family purse?"

"I'm not that degenerate," I muttered, resenting the truth behind his insinuation.

"Could've fooled me."

He turned, with his eyes meeting mine, glinting with something between amusement and intimidation. "Wait here."

He approached the captain's quarters, then pounded on the cabin door before pushing it open. When the door swung open, I caught a glimpse of Mr. Bellamy, seated at his desk, with a tankard raised toward his mouth.

"What are you doing!?" Bellamy's voice was edged with irritation.

Then the door shut, muffling the words that followed.

As I stood by waiting, I observed the ships in the harbor. A vessel tied to the wharf drew my eye with her towering masts stretching skyward as though to brush the clouds.

"Who owns that ship?" I asked one of the crew.

The sailor leaned towards me. "That's the latest addition to the Standard Shipping Co.'s fleet. Built nearby in Medford."

"A fine ship," I muttered, still contemplating its purpose. "Though too small for a voyage to China or Europe."

"It's meant for the West Indies."

The Standard Shipping Co. already had become one of the predominant shipping companies, shipping goods to and from Europe and China. Their expansion into the West Indies spelled trouble for those already involved in that trade route.

"At this rate, they're going to take over the whole shipping industry."

"Right, lad. Competition is fierce," he said, his countenance serious.

A few moments later, John reappeared, stepping out with that crooked smile of his.

"Good luck, he isn't nice when he has been drinking" he murmured, waving me inside.

I stepped into the dimly lit cabin, its cramped, unwelcoming confines making me more apprehensive. The windows were small, casting narrow beams of light across the cluttered desk with a ledger already open containing a long list of names and balances due. Despite his ugly reputation, he didn't look the part. He was tall and broad-shouldered. His navy wool jacket was crisp, his white cuffs spotless. But for all his fine attire, there was something about him that warned even the most reckless man against crossing him. He locked in a deep stare before speaking.

"You're here to pay me?"

"Yes, sir," I muttered.

I reached into my pocket, withdrew the bag of shillings, and set it down on his desk with a slight thud. He arched an eyebrow, then untied the bag, his fingers moving with practiced efficiency as he counted, the clank of coins filling the silence. When he finished counting, he leaned back in his chair. He looked at me, searching for answers.

"Tell me…how did you come by this?"

"I sold something that belonged to me," I said simply. "We're even, right?

"Well…I suppose."

"You suppose? It's all there. Plus interest!"

"I speak in jest, young man. But now that you have proven creditworthy…any desire to borrow more?"

I considered his offer, as unreasonable as it might have seemed. A part of me wanted to get the books back, while another part of me wanted to drink and gamble. But having to face him or John again was not in my cards for now.

"I will have to decline. Good day."

He gave me a curt nod, and I left.

The encounter caused my hand to tremble. To my disdain, John was lounging against the ship's side on the quarterdeck.

"Well, look at that," he mused. "You made it out alive. No bad blood, right, lad?"

"Right," I mumbled, brushing past him.

As I exited the ship, I quickened my pace. My veins surged with a nervous heat, as though I had just gotten into a conflict, when reality was, I had settled my debt. Though the burden of my debt was gone, a hollow unease settled in my stomach. The kind that no amount of money could erase. Those books were more than text. They were memories of my father, relics of a time before debts, before desperation, before the grim notion that nothing would ever be simple again.

Later that evening, at supper, the family gathered around the large oak dining table, its surface worn smooth by years of joyful and at other times contentious conversations. The fire in the hearth snapped and hissed, filling the kitchen and parlor with the comfort of familiarity. Laid out before us was the usual dinner: boiled and salted cod, potatoes with butter, and turnips. The routine, the familiarity only made me more eager. I wasn't built for it. I remained quiet, waiting for an opportunity to break the monotony.

"The Fourth of July is but ten days away," I said, my fork pausing mid-air.

Mother nodded, lips pressed thin. "Yes. A selectman came by the house today, inquiring if we might contribute toward the fireworks display this year."

"What did you tell him?" Jameson pressed.

"I told him we would have to give it thought," she said, glancing sideways.

I leaned forward. "We should donate this year. Father has always taken pride in this tradition. The least we can do is keep it while he is away."

My mother studied me, her brow furrowing. "I agree with your sentiment, Caleb, but with him being gone, don't you think we should be more prudent?"

"Since no one has come to claim the indigo yet, we can sell it and use the funds from that. I can handle the arrangements."

"What's come over you? You've never been this…what's the word…conscientious," Charlotte said, promptly holding her hand over her mouth.

Unshaken, I met her eyes. "I simply believe we should honor Father's tradition."

Her smirk faded. "Maybe you are right."

"If you are so insistent, then we shall contribute," my mother interjected, though I could tell she was not convinced it was the best action to take.

With my debt settled and the Fourth of July approaching, I now had something to look forward to. Especially since Maryann was going to be at the celebration.

Chapter 8 (June) – Loyalties in Question

After we successfully sold the indigo, I made the family donation to the town officials for the Fourth of July celebration. I had scarcely placed the money in their hands before they presumed to ask if I might lend my time in setting up as well. Though my patience was thinning, I agreed to participate. At least I'd see Maryann soon, I thought. The notion lingered, offering a rare moment of reprieve in a week otherwise muddled by mounting burdens.

I sat down in the counting room, reluctantly tallying accounts and grappling with the company's true standing, between what was owed, what lay ahead. That afternoon, as I jammed an ink-laden quill into the ledger's next empty column, fresh trouble greeted me with a hard knock on the door.

"Come in."

Captain Ewan entered abruptly. The deep lines near his eyes hinted at hard-fought battles and nights of raucous laughter. This time, his expression was lined with concern. "I don't suppose you've heard?"

"Heard what?" I asked, bracing for the answer.

"The crew of the *Friendship*…near the whole lot of 'em…failed to turn up this morning to load her cargo."

I stared at him. "What? Why?"

"Not spoken by me, but by them. They vowed they would not serve a traitor."

A sharp laugh escaped me, though there was no humor in it. "A traitor?"

Ewan's face tightened. "Word is going 'round that your father was a Loyalist during the war."

My breath hitched. "That is absolutley absurd! That can't be."

Ewan lifted a shoulder. "Truth be what it may, the men are gone. Some have gone to work for Mr. Bellamy. The rest abandoned us, convinced we would never put to sea."

I exhaled sharply, clenching my fists. "Perhaps I can speak to them."

"You may try. But, Caleb…" His voice lowered. "…if you don't bring them round, I'll be gone myself."

His words were harsh. He was a good, respected man who meant what he said. I immediately got up and made my way down the wharf toward one of Mr. Bellamy's ships, while Captain Ewan waited near the *Friendship*. When I approached the ship, I spotted former crew members loading cargo. Spotting Silas among them, I called his name. But he pretended not to hear me. So, I strode forward into his view until avoidance was no longer an option.

"After all these years," I yelled out, "you leave over a rumor?"

He came to the edge of the ship. "I don't like it either, lad. But your father's name was on a document, clear as day."

"Document…what document?"

"One of the lads received a letter, said to be from a man of Satucket, who claimed to have known your father. That letter was passed about and with it a roll of those marked as Loyalist Associators in the war. His name was there among the rest."

I shook my head. "The document must have been forged!"

"It is not only that. In your father's absence, the men have little confidence in the business's future. And we've had offers of equal wages besides."

My gut heaved like a mad ocean, but before I could press further, I saw John approaching. That alone was enough to repel me back toward the *Friendship*, only to find that Ewan, too, had vanished. The entire crew was gone. Now, their captain too. I was left standing there, blindsided by how quickly things were breaking down without my father around. But the accusations were the most troubling. So, I hurried home in a state of worry.

When I reached the house, I went to the backyard, where my mother and sisters were hanging linens on a line. Their conversation hushed the moment they saw me rushing over, my eyes wide and darting.

"Caleb, what is it?" Mother asked.

"The crew of the *Friendship* has quit," I replied, my voice taut with frustration. "Ewan as well."

Mother gripped the linen in her hand. "What? Why?!"

I paused. Everything I thought I knew had just been flipped upside down. "They believe Father was a Loyalist."

For a moment, the only sound was the faint flap of fabric caught in the wind. Then, quietly, my mother asked, "Where did they hear such a thing?"

"A document circulated amongst the men with his name amongst a list of Loyalists."

I expected indignation, a firm denial. Instead, her gaze drifted downward, as though searching for words that would not come. My anger quickened, my blood rising with a furious boil. I couldn't just ignore what was happening.

"You knew about this!"

"Of course not," she answered quickly. But her voice wavered. Without another word, she turned and disappeared into the house. The linen she had been holding lay rumpled on the ground.

I had always thought of my father as a demanding, exacting and unyielding man. But the idea of him being a Loyalist was unthinkable. Seeking solitude, I wandered to the Charles River's bridge and stood at the center, questioning the past and doubting the future. The bridge itself was just a few years old and had become a vital link between Boston and Cambridge, stretching across what had once been open water and marsh. The river flowed steadily on the surface, but the turbulence beneath was a hidden current, like the blood that pounded through my veins. Sloops and fishing boats drifted toward the harbor, their sails catching the last golden light of the day. At the ropewalk, men paced backward, tugging fiercely, twisting fibers into taut lengths of twine. So too were the knots coiling in my stomach, tightening, twisting like strained fibers as I thought about the rumors.

I watched the rhythm of the maritime activities, remembering how my father, brother, and I would come here to escape the summer's heat at the river, to fish, to sit in silence and observe. But now it felt hollow, as though those moments were a dream. I could not believe the news about my father. Would not. For years, I lived under the shadow of his expectations with his virtues and reputation ever eclipsing my own shortcomings. But now, I wasn't sure what I believed. I wasn't sure if I had ever really known him at all. The sun began to sink lower when Jameson appeared beside me.

"I knew I would find you here, brother."

"What do you want?" I asked, avoiding eye contact.

"What's happened?"

"The whole crew of the *Friendship* quit."

"The whole crew?"

"The whole crew. But that's the least of it."

"Is it true? Was Father a Loyalist?"

I looked at him intently. "Apparently so. Mother's response was quite telling… She wouldn't answer me when I asked her about it."

Jameson's brow furrowed. "Do you think she knows something?"

I exhaled slowly. "It sure appears that way. You know, we were young when we left Satucket. I hardly remember it. But maybe this is why we left. To escape his ties…"

Jameson outstretched his arms. "What are we going to do now?"

"Get to the bottom of these rumors," I said, hanging my head in my hand.

We stood in silence as dusk settled over the treetops beyond the far bank. The pressure was mounting, and cracks were forming on the surface. Without the *Friendship's* crew, we were in danger of losing the ship altogether. With my father's absence and reputation being questioned, we stood to lose much more. Jameson studied me briefly as I remained in a trance, then turned his eyes to the river with its never-ceasing current.

Chapter 9 (June) –
Secrets of the Past

Later that night, as the house settled into the hush of slumber, I lay awake, my mind clouded with unanswered questions like a ship lost in the fog. The scent of spent tallow clung to the room's stillness while I stared at the ceiling. Unable to stand the wait any longer, I slipped from bed, my bare feet meeting the cool wooden floor.

As I descended the stairs, they groaned beneath, each step threatening to give me away. I paused, listening. Nothing but silence, so I continued carefully like a thief in the night.

I grabbed the cellar key, lit the lantern candle near the front door using the remnants of a fire from the hearth, and began my careful exit. The front door yielded with practiced ease, the latch catching softly as I slowly shut it. The street lay bathed in a silver hue of moonlight. I stayed as quiet as possible, slipping quickly to the cellar doors located just to the right side of the house. I unlocked the wooden doors and pulled them open. The doors didn't just resist; they warned me. But with effort, they gave way revealing the black mouth of the cellar and the secrets kept within. The damp air from below was earthy, laced with mildew and time. Holding the lantern carefully, I descended the stone steps.

Barrels and crates lined the walls, their contents of preserved food and vegetables accounted for. I moved gingerly, scanning the area until my eyes landed on my father's wooden chest shoved against the far wall. Kneeling, I traced my fingers over its rough surface. An uninvited thought came to mind, to turn around and head back upstairs. But it was too late. I had to know more. I opened the chest, anticipating that what lay inside would change everything. The hinges groaned as I pried the chest open, the past now mine to discover. I stood back, the lantern revealing a scattering of relics: a double-breasted coarse wool navy-blue coat, the scent of pipe smoke still present. Then I grabbed what appeared to be a miniature octant, one used for mapping, worn smooth from use. There was a peculiar single plain piece of paper that had an oval shape cut out in its middle and an intriguing wooden device fitted with numerous small spinning wheels, each marked with scattered letters. There was also a bundle of letters, their parchment brittle with age. I looked at each item one by one. The shadows now all had faces as I looked around to make sure no one was there. Eerily, it was like my father was present, yet he clearly wasn't. Beneath it all, something cold met my fingers. I hesitated, then pulled it free to discover a pistol! I hung the lantern over it, the light revealing its surface, the metal dull with time yet unmistakable in its form. Turning it over, I found the familiar marking of a broad arrow, stamped into the steel. It was clearly British property with that mark! My stomach clenched. My father had no reason to possess such a weapon, not unless…

Breathing hard, I turned back to the box and reached for the letters. My hands trembled as I sifted through them, searching for meaning. Then, among the brittle pages, I found something else: a newspaper article, its edges yellowed with time. The headline read:

Unfortunate Blaze Kills Two in Boston

We regret to inform our readers of a most lamentable incident that occurred late Saturday evening on Winter Street. It is reported that an unruly mob, inflamed by resentments lingering since the close of the late war, descended upon the dwelling of Mr. Smith, a modest tradesman of respectable character.

Eyewitnesses describe the rioters as armed with clubs and torches, their shouts filling the night. Despite pleas for mercy from neighbors, they set fire to the premises, which were soon entirely consumed.

Tragically, two persons, Mr. Nathaniel Smith and his wife, Mrs. Elizebeth Smith, perished in the flames. Mrs. Smith suffocated from smoke, while her husband, Nathaniel, burned trying to save her. Neighbors attempted in vain to rescue them, the heat and smoke proving insurmountable. Their remains were recovered only after dawn, a scene of most affecting horror. Their young son survived.

Authorities have promised a full inquiry into the origins of the riot and the culpability of its leaders. At present, no arrests have been announced.

We lament that the spirit of violence, so lately thought extinguished with the return of peace, should again show itself in such savage form. We commend to the attention of our magistrates the necessity of vigilance, lest the miseries of war continue to visit us in this shocking manner.

I laid the article down, sorrow filling my heart to the point I wanted to discover no more. I took a deep breath and scarcely scanned more documents; my eyes caught a familiar name on a letter: *Mr. Hall.* My father had once called him a friend. Then, without explanation, they'd parted ways. I read fragments of a letter where Mr. Hall pleaded to meet with my father, asking for a chance to talk. I shuffled through more pages and letters. All from Mr. Hall. The feeling in my stomach sank deeper. This was no simple falling out. This was something else. Something precarious. Gathering what I could, the pistol, the coat and the letters, I hurried back up the steps. As I shut the cellar doors, it was as though something had changed deep within me. Secrets, long buried, had found their way to the surface.

Early the following morning, while I stood at the kitchen entrance, the gravity of last night's discovery pressed down on me. There was a heavy scent of baking bread, the hearth crackling with quiet consistency. My mother was at the counter preparing ham, her hands moving in steady, familiar motions. She knew I was there, yet she kept on with the preparations.

"If Father wasn't a Loyalist," I blurted, breaking the unbearable silence, "then why did he have a pistol marked with a Broad Arrow?"

Her hands faltered, just for a moment. "You went through his things."

"Yes…and unfortunately, they confirm the rumors."

She exhaled, shaking her head, but she did not look at me. "This isn't something I wish to discuss at the moment."

"Why are you keeping things from me?"

She continued to prepare breakfast.

My chest tensed with frustration. "Why did Mr. Hall and Father stop speaking?"

She became completely still, then she wiped her hands on her apron and turned, her expression unembellished.

"They were friends once; then they weren't."

I searched her face, searching for something: an admission, a denial. But she calmly turned back to her task, gathering the plates. Her words settled over me, but more with what they did not say. There was no explanation from her. Yet the past was no longer distant. It had form now, some meaning and I was doubtful I was ready for what I would find the deeper I went.

Chapter 10 (July) – Fourth of July

When the Fourth of July finally arrived, I left the house, eager to swiftly finish my volunteer work and join the festivities so that I could connect with Maryann. The sky was cloudless and clear with the sun covering every inch of the harbor. As I worked alongside other volunteers adorning ships with red, white, and blue buntings and setting up the mortar for the evening's illumination, my eyes lingered on the *Friendship*. Now decommissioned, its decks empty, its fate sealed by men who had walked away rather than labor under my father's questionable name.

When my volunteer duties concluded, I turned and paused to take in the view of the harbor. Snapping in the summer breeze, countless flags spread out over the harbor bearing fifteen stars with alternating red and white stripes. The grand sight of merchant and navy ships, adorned with red, white, and blue banners and flags, made me proud.

After observing the harbor, I made my way to State Street where the festivities were beginning to take place. The town was decked for festivity, with ribbons and American flags displayed from the eaves of busy shops and houses of trade, from counting rooms and coffee houses to the law offices and print shops that lined the way on both sides of the street. It had been nearly thirty years since the British were expelled after an eleven-month siege. Through turbulence that followed, Boston at last began to discern its promise. On this day, the streets swelled with pride and expectation.

I made my way farther up the street towards the Old State House, whereas in tradition, the morning began with an oration with processions of militia and citizens to follow. Townspeople lined the cobblestone-laden street, admiring and gleaming with anticipation as they waited for the parade to commence. As I searched for a better vantage point, I passed by the local shoemaker, Mr. Brown. I gave him a nod, but he dismissed me outright. For a moment, I figured that he simply hadn't recognized me. But then a deep wariness took hold. I realized the rumors about my father must have spread.

Militia, in crisp formation, displaying banners emblazoned with distinctive emblems representing their distinctive regiments, marched to the sounds of fife and drum. The spirit of patriotism was palpable, but as I continued walking among the crowd, the presence of silent judgment hovered over me. I spotted more familiar faces, still none acknowledging me. Slowly, I began to regret the volunteer work I did. If the town intended to judge me by my father's tarnished past, I preferred to keep my distance. As I departed the area, I recognized a man walking nearby.

Mr. Hall was a distinguished man who had an air of authority as he strolled arm in arm with his wife. I wondered if he would recognize me if I approached. But that didn't matter. The opportunity presented itself too loudly. I approached regardless of what his potential reaction might be. I weaved through the throng of people, my heart pounding feverishly as I caught up to him.

"Excuse me, Mr. Hall!?"

He turned slowly. A flash of tension tightened his brow as his eyes narrowed upon me. Then, as recognition set in, his mouth eased, and the lines around his eyes relaxed. "Ah, Caleb. How are you?"

"To be honest…troubled," I replied. "Might I have a moment to speak with you?"

He was quiet for a short moment. He looked at his wife then back at me. "Of course".

His wife grinned, then stepped away.

"I'm sorry to hear of your father's conscription."

"Thank you. It has been challenging, to say the least… I was hoping you might help me understand him better. There are rumors claiming he was a Loyalist."

Mr. Hall's face hardened. "A Loyalist?" He shook his head. "Let me assure you, he was not."

"How can you be certain?" I pressed. "A man from Satucket circulated a document saying he was."

The crowd began to roar in cheer and adulation as some veterans of the war, dressed in Continental Army uniforms passed.

Mr. Hall sighed, his posture stiffening. He waited for the crowd noise to simmer. "Caleb, as a lawyer, my work demands precision based on facts. I do not know this man from Satucket, who sounds rather suspicious to me, nor his connection to your father. But I can tell you with certainty that your father was no Loyalist. That is the truth."

His tone was final, but I persisted. "If I could ask you one more thing?"

"Go ahead."

"Why did my father stop speaking to you?"

His eyes drifted downwards, then back to me. "There are events in life best left untouched," he said finally. "Some things are not meant to be revisited. I must rejoin my wife and the festivities. I wish you well." He tipped his hat and returned to his wife.

Perplexed, I departed from the area, heading to the Common, where my family was stationed. I didn't know what to believe, between the recent rumors and what Mr. Hall told me. Mr. Hall was convincing with his tone. He wasn't for lying. Maybe he was defending my father's honor. But that was not how he presented his answer. He seemed angered. I continued to walk, when I came to the open green fields of the Common, filled with families dressed in their finest attire, men in tailcoats, women in silk gowns, and children dressed like miniatures of their parents. Scattered stately oaks, graceful elms, and vibrant maple trees provided a natural canopy for some. I searched amongst the people and spotted my family where we normally conjugated.

"Where's Mother?" I asked.

"She decided to rest," Charlotte replied.

"Is she ill?"

"No, she said she was just not feeling up to it."

Jameson and my sisters, oblivious to the undercurrent of disapproval towards my father, darted off to join their friends. Their togetherness only deepened my own sense of isolation. There was a small band playing rousing tunes, vendors selling simple refreshments and delectable snacks, families setting up picnics while children played tag and chase. But my father's absence and my mother's distance occupied my thoughts.

Soon my friend Owen appeared, his usual grin lighting up my mood. He was the only person I trusted, perhaps because he earned it by his persistence. He always kept his word, and even when I had made a fool of myself at the tavern countless times, he never stopped being my friend. Only a few weeks before, when I'd come up short on my tab, Owen placed a shilling quietly on the counter and steered me home without a lecture. Together, we roamed the trodden paths of the Common, observing the crowds and activities.

"You seem a bit low, Caleb."

"Well, it's been a bit topsy-turvy."

"Do tell."

I cleared my throat. "If you haven't heard, there are rumors about my father being a Loyalist during the war."

"I must admit I have."

"I am sure the whole town knows now. I can tell by the looks people are giving me. At any rate, I ran into my father's friend, and he told me quite emphatically that my father was not a Loyalist."

"Wow, that is quite a turn of events."

"I know. But I don't know what to believe. Mainly, because I went through my father's belongings and found a British pistol."

"That would give anyone pause."

"Yes, very. My mother, who I thought could give me clarity, only made it more unclear. And now this."

"Well, my friend. No matter what, I am here for you," Owen said, his smile bringing comfort to my divided mind.

"I ought not to complain," I said after a moment. "Not when I considered your own circumstances."

Owen gave a faint smile though it did not reach his eyes.

"Think nothing of it, Caleb. I have made my way well enough." He paused, then added more quietly, "There was little choice in it. When a family has not the means, a boy is soon placed where he may earn his keep."

Eventually, Owen and I found an empty area on the grass. We slumped onto the grass, observing the joyous crowd. My search for Maryann had thus far proven fruitless, and I doubted if I would ever cross paths with her. As we continued to hold conversation, I was preoccupied by thoughts of my father's plight and his surfacing past, now about to resign myself to the disappointing feeling my efforts had been in vain. None of it seemed to matter now, between my volunteering and the donation. But then, I spotted Maryann with others her age just within our line of sight. She stood at the massive elm tree at the center of the Common. And she had seemingly been looking our way. Owen's eyes flickered as he pointed toward the group.

"There's my cousin Catherine," he said as he gathered himself and stood.

My pulse quickened. The sight of Maryann sent a joyous jolt through me, snapping me out of my despondency. But even better, Owen's cousin knew her. Owen led the way, and I followed, eager yet uncertain. As we approached, their laughter was loud and contagious.

"Looks like you've been at some exclusive gathering," Owen teased.

"Oh, it was wonderful! The food and the company were fantastic," Catherine said with a smile.

"For those of you who don't know, this is Caleb," Owen said, nudging me forward.

I bowed, and the young women offered polite curtsies.

Maryann stepped forward from the group, her expression bright. "I'm glad to see you here," she said, touching my shoulder lightly.

"The sentiment is mutual," I replied, trying to match her warmth.

"Maryann, you know it's unseemly to touch a young gentleman in public," one of her friends quietly teased.

"Oh relax, I know him," Maryann replied, looking at her friend.

I took a breath, gathering my courage. "I spent the morning helping with the mortar for the show this evening," I explained. "My family donated to the festivities. They'll be launching the rockets from the harbor."

Maryann's eyes sparkled. "I've been looking forward to it all day."

Encouraged, I continued, "And how have you been enjoying the celebration?"

"We spent most of the afternoon at my house," she replied. "Guests, food…the usual banter."

"And what convinced you to join the common folk?" I joked.

Laughter rippled through the group, the conversation flowing easily. But before my confidence remained high, I noticed an unfamiliar fellow coming towards the group. He was sharply dressed, with an impeccable navy-blue tailcoat and a fob watch tucked into it. He certainly appeared to be wealthy for his youth. He was tall and slender with a self-assured demeanor, his brown hair and warm brown eyes adding to his charm.

Owen leaned in. "That's Charles Derby. He's courting Maryann."

The words hit me like a cold bucket of ocean water. I felt an unease so strong I wanted to leave, my posture drooping, my spirit discouraged.

The others shifted, making space for him.

"Are we ready to get a spot in the harbor for the illuminations?" Charles asked, his voice carrying over the chatter, demanding attention.

The group walked toward the harbor, with Maryann following closely beside him. But I had no formal introduction. As the group walked, I slowed my steps, watching them drift ahead. Owen stopped and came back to meet me, concern written across his face.

"I've got to attend to something," I murmured.

Owen hesitated before nodding, then caught up with the others. Feeling defeated, I had to get my mind straight. I made my way toward The Green Dragon Tavern. Regretful and disheartened by the day's event, I sat in the tavern while the festivities continued. The day had worn on me, from being burdened by my father's maligned reputation, to Mr. Hall's adamant denial of such rumors, to seeing Maryann, then learning she was being courted by someone far superior to me. As I drank my tankard of ale, I heard fireworks beginning to crackle outside, with the town cheering as the illuminations erupted. But all I could picture was the light reflecting in Maryann's eyes as she sat beside someone else.

Chapter 11 (July) – Surfacing Revelations

After I fully recovered from the overabundance of ale I had taken in, I sat in the family counting room attempting to catch up on the accounts. Though I was thoroughly distracted. The oppressive heat settled over the town like an unwelcome guest as I contemplated what Mr. Hall said to me on the Fourth of July. His words had taken root, and I could not shake them. There was no hesitation when he said my father was not a Loyalist. He meant it with every fiber of his being. Yet if my father was not a Loyalist but had been in possession of British property and named among the ranks of their supporters, there was only one explanation. The realization struck with such force that I pushed myself back from the desk and rushed home to quickly snatch the letters bearing Mr. Hall's name, along with other documents belonging to my father. Once I gathered enough of my father's belongings, I hurried to Mr. Hall's office on Court Street, near the Old State House.

When I arrived, I knocked hard and with conviction.

Then the door opened. Mr. Hall's face was lined with weariness, conveying his disapproval. "Son, I thought I made it clear that I would not entertain more discussion."

"You were right, Mr. Hall. My father was not a Loyalist," I said, my voice steady. "He was a spy."

For a moment, he just stood there silently. "Caleb, I must get back to my work," he said as he slowly began to close the door.

But I stuck my foot in his door, and I could still see his face. Then, a small, knowing smile tugged at the corners of his mouth.

"All right, you've figured it out," he murmured as he stepped aside, gesturing for me to enter.

I stepped inside quickly before he could change his mind as he walked to his desk.

"What did he do?" I pressed, taking a seat.

Mr. Hall leaned forward and folded his arms on his desk.

"Your father worked for George Washington."

"Did you serve with him?" I asked, my heart pounding from the anticipation of where this was all going.

"Not directly," he admitted. "But we met when he came to Boston during the siege. We became contacts. Over time, we became friends."

I handed him the documents I had brought. As he leafed through them, his expression darkened when he reached a particular page. He exhaled slowly and set it down.

"Your father carried a heavy burden," he said, his voice barely above a whisper.

"What do you mean?"

He stalled before speaking again. "Your father infiltrated Loyalist circles, pretending to be one of them, gathering intelligence."

"So then, that explains why he was on a list of Loyalists' associators."

"Precisely."

"But who was that man who spread those rumors?"

Mr. Hall gave me a blank look and shook his head.

My eyes focused on the article he set down. "And that?"

Mr. Hall looked pained. "Caleb, I think we should stop here."

"I won't," I said, my voice firm. "I need to know more."

For a long moment, he studied me, as if weighing my resolve. He leaned back in his chair, his gaze fixed on the ceiling as if the past played out there, just beyond his reach. Then, he sighed and continued, "It's a tragic story, I'm warning."

"Please carry on."

"During the war, as the British lay siege to Boston, the town became divided between those who were loyal and those who were against the crown. Many Patriots left town to escape the threat from the occupying army. Eventually, after eleven months, the British left. When the British evacuated, many of the Patriots returned, while many Loyalists fled, fearing for their own safety. The ones who remained in town assimilated themselves among the Patriots. Yet there was still hostility towards them. Soon after the war, your father recognized one such Loyalist who had been deeply entrenched with the British forces during the siege. One evening, he confided his findings to me, and that information, Caleb, fell into the wrong hands." He hesitated, working up the strength to continue. "A mob consumed with vengeance, acted without thought or restraint. They confronted the Loyalist in his home. In the chaos, the house was set ablaze. Inside, the man and his wife perished. Only their young son survived."

My eyes drifted towards the floor, then slowly back to Mr. Hall. "My father wasn't involved, was he?"

"No," he replied firmly. "But he blamed himself. He carried the guilt for years, believing that he was responsible for their deaths."

I sat in stunned silence. "How did the information leak?"

Mr. Hall's shoulders slumped, his composure faltering. He looked down, his hands clasped together, then inhaled deeply.

"It was my doing," he admitted, his voice thick with seriousness. "A young woman I was seeing at the time overheard our conversation, the evening your father divulged this information to me. She passed the information along, naming your father as the source." He sighed heavily. "I take full responsibility. I should have been more careful."

"You did not deliberately leak the information."

He shook his head. "Perhaps. But there's more to it. The woman…she was not my wife. It was an affair, and I was reckless."

I absorbed his words, then asked quietly, "Where did the fire happen?"

"Winter Street," he said. "There is an empty lot where the house once stood."

The significance of his recollection settled over us. We sat in silence for a few moments. With no more questions arising, I got out of the chair to leave, collecting the documents.

"You wouldn't happen to know of the name Mr. Prescott, do you?"

"I am sorry, no."

"What about the New England Mercantile Co.?"

"Never heard of that establishment. Why do you ask?"

"It seems no one has. It's really nothing. Thank you for your time, Mr. Hall. May I visit again?"

He nodded, his expression now filled with somberness rather than the naturally serious look he carried. "Of course. Caleb, your father is a good man. And I hope he returns home safely."

I stepped out into the street, the newly acquired knowledge changing my understanding of the world. I knew now that my father was a spy working for George Washington and the reason for the fallout between Mr. Hall and him. While this was deeply revealing, I still felt empty.

I visited Winter Street, driven by a restless need to understand more. As I approached the empty lot, I slowed, my thoughts echoing the words from the article: *Elizabeth Smith suffocated from smoke, her husband, Nathaniel, burned trying to save her.*

The lot was barren, a stark contrast against the mixed rows of surrounding clapboard and Federal-style brick homes. As I stood there, lost in thought, a man stopped by.

"No one will buy that lot," he remarked. "People say it's cursed."

"Did you know the family?" I asked.

"Not directly, no. But I knew of 'em. A decent God-fearing family. Caught in the middle of the war like the rest of us," he admitted. "A cruel end, it was. Left a young boy behind."

"Devastating," I said, the gravity of the fragmented scene playing out in my imagination.

He nodded toward the cemetery down the road. "The Smiths' graves are in the Old Granary Burying Ground."

Though the Smiths were buried, the reminders of them made it seem they hadn't left at all.

"I should be getting home. Good day, sir."

But even as I said that, I knew I wouldn't be heading home. The burden of the past was too heavy to ignore. I made my way to the burial ground, where beyond the iron fencing, rows of tombstones stretched long in the dimming sunlight. I searched the stones, passing by a notable name: *Saml Adams, born 1722…died 1803.* My father was fond of Mr. Adams, speaking often of his willingness to sacrifice for the greater good. I continued to scan the tombstones, afraid to find the names I was looking for, yet needing to confirm it was all real. Then among the weathered stones, I found what I sought: *Nathaniel Smith, born 1753…died 1785. Elizabeth Smith, born 1755…died 1785.* And then I noticed something strange. There were partly withered white roses resting against the headstones, as though someone had been there recently. A chill went through me as I stood there. I told myself it shouldn't matter. It was in the past, and I wasn't the one who did it. Yet for all that I had brought to light, I remained bound to the burden of this wretched misfortune, and the shadow it cast upon my father, Mr. Hall, and the town.

Chapter 12 (July) – Secrets Remain

When I returned home, the house was steeped in silence, every shadow elongated by the glow of the setting sun. My supper sat on the dinner table, cold and unappealing, while my sisters cleaned the dishes and tidied the kitchen without any conversation. I passed by them, in no mood for chatter. I found my mother already in bed. Typically, she would have been up reading or sipping coffee with a friend.

For a moment, I wanted to demand answers. We had hardly spoken since I admitted to looking through my father's belongings. But now, I was closer to the truth. I questioned if perhaps she, too, had been unaware of the secrets I had uncovered or worse, she knew and was harboring them to protect the family from feeling their torment.

I ascended the stairs slowly, each step measured. Halfway up, her voice broke the silence between us.

"Caleb, is everything all right?"

A torrent of emotion surged within me from sorrow to a strong sense of frustration I could barely contain. I turned around and walked to the door of her dimly candlelit bedroom.

"Did you know that Father was a spy?" I inquired in a tone that was respectful but deliberate.

For a long moment, she offered no reply. The rift between us seemed to widen into a vast chasm as I waited. Finally, she exhaled and confessed. "Yes. I knew."

"Then why did you lie to me?" I asked, my voice barely masking my disappointment.

She sat up and looked at me intently. "Please keep your voice low."

I shook my head, then approached her bedside. "Why, so no one can hear the truth?"

"Your father wished for these things to be kept secret."

"Such as the family that was killed in the fire?"

Her face became expressionless. Her voice shook as she spoke, "Yes. He bore that burden…so you and your siblings would never feel the deep sorrow he held."

A moment went by as the reality of her words settled.

"I spoke with Mr. Hall today. He revealed many things about Father's past. I visited the lot where the house once stood…and the gravesite."

She rested her hand on my shoulder, tightening her grip in a silent comfort. "I am sorry you had to learn of these tragic events. But you know your father did not kill those people," she said, her voice tender yet firm.

"Yes, of course. I understand why he felt guilty and wanted it to be in the past. I wish I could have ignored it all too," I admitted, "but I felt compelled to know the truth. I just don't understand why you kept all this from us while those rumors were going around."

"Had he been here, I cannot judge how he would have faced those rumors. But he is not, and I will not betray what I know to be his wishes."

"I noticed something odd at the cemetery. There were flowers on the graves of Mr. and Mrs. Smith. They looked near fresh, as if someone had just placed them there."

Her brow furrowed thoughtfully. "That is quite odd."

"I thought so too," I replied softly. "Perhaps a friend or a mourner pays them homage?"

"Possibly," she murmured, "let us pray for your father's return. And for now, let's keep this between us."

I nodded, then retraced my steps back up the stairs, the spirit of our shared secrets now a presence in the house. As I climbed into bed, my thoughts churned. Was uncovering these matters worth the pain, or might ignorance have been kinder? Yet still, who was that man from Satucket who labeled my Father a Loyalist, knowing full well it was a lie? The search for answers was as inexorable as the ocean's current, and I was already caught in its relentless pull. Too many pieces of the puzzle were missing. With my mind unready to rest, I lit a candle and opened my father's personal journal. Though I did not find him writing about his days as a spy, entry after entry was compelling. From tales of relentless storms and trades gone wrong, it was like stepping into a real-life *Robinson Crusoe* or *Gulliver's Travels*, only these adventures actually happened. I continued into the night, my thirst to read more unquenchable, until exhaustion overtook me and I surrendered to sleep.

Chapter 13 (August) –
Erosions

The weeks that followed, the house, once alive with the gentle hum of domestic routine, now lay desolate, as if belaboring my father's absence. One morning, my mother sat at the parlor table, with a crisp copy of the *Boston Gazette* in front of her. The afternoon light, beaming and unyielding, seeped through the weary cracks in the kitchen shutters. I leaned over, and read a headline on the newspaper:

Tensions Rise Between Napoleon and the Royal Navy

The words intensified the more pressing query that pulsed in my mind: Where was my father? Was he in danger amidst the turmoil of the Napoleonic War? The ink had long dried on the page, leaving no chance for further revision, much like the irreversible decisions that had marked our lives. What if he had not endeavored past his normal route?

"Anything interesting in the paper?" I inquired.

My mother hesitated, a practiced neutrality masking the tumult beneath. "Nothing too interesting," she replied, carefully folding the paper as if to shield me from the relentless reminder of our misfortune. "By the way, we've had a reply to the advertisement for the *Friendship*. Will you meet the man at the American Coffee House?"

Ironically, she was the one who suggested the idea to sell the sloop, given we could not hire a new crew to replace the one that left.

"I don't know… I don't like the idea of selling it."

"I know. I feel the same way. But we have no choice. We cannot keep an empty ship while we pay fees to harbor it."

"Why can't you go?"

"Caleb, look at me. I am in disarray. I would portray desperation."

"Who am I to meet?" I inquired, already feeling the weight of responsibility and the hope this could turn things around for us financially.

"Mr. Williams is his name. He is a prosperous man from Newport. You'll find him at the coffee house, three o'clock sharp."

Though I wanted little to do with all the burdens my father's business carried, this was different. This was his first sloop.

"The sum was set at two thousand two hundred. Just be sure that you hold firm above nineteen hundred," she replied, her tone leaving no room for negotiation.

I murmured a reluctant assent. As my sisters set off for the market, I lingered a moment in the parlor, contemplating the ramifications of the task at hand. If we had the means, we would not be selling the sloop. Its absence would erode not only our ability to ship goods to the West Indies but our status. Yet if I made the deal happen, maybe I could prove my ability to manage the family business. And if by chance, with fortune taking a turn for the good, we could regain another sloop or larger vessel when my father returned.

When time finally beckoned, I departed with a singular, determined purpose to secure a sale that would, in some measure, help us to endure. I made my way to the American Coffee House, each step weighted with the knowledge I was not only negotiating a deal but confronting my long-held trepidation towards competence and responsibility. This particular coffee house was one where my father would often frequent in order to meet with merchants, to reckon terms, and bring contracts to their close. The place pleased him greatly, for he would remind us that coffee was the American's chosen draught since the Tea Act had made tea a badge of loyalty to the Crown.

Inside, the establishment exuded a buzzing network of people from merchants to shopkeepers to townspeople busy about deals or politics. Lamps filled with whale-oil flickered dancing light against paneled walls. The rich aroma of roasted coffee mingled with the murmurs of whispered deals. In one shadowed corner, a cluster of merchants pored over faded maps and ledger books, their deep voices an undercurrent to the vibrant energy of their surroundings. I made my way to the wide pine coffee-counter stationed in the rear where the master poured bittersweet coffee from a copper urn.

"I'm here to meet Mr. Williams at three o'clock."

"Are you Caleb Thompson?"

"Yes, that's correct."

"Mr. Williams is already here," he said, pointing towards a table.

I was surprised. I was a bit early, but Mr. Williams had already been waiting. I quickly walked over, his stoic countenance telling me I was in for a tough negotiation.

"Caleb?" he asked, setting aside his pocket watch.

"Yes. Mr. Williams?"

He put out his stout hand, "Nice to meet you. I have to be somewhere later this evening and don't have a lot of time to waste."

I sat down, my anxieties beginning to flourish. He looked at me with anticipation, quill pen in hand, ready to write in his pocketbook.

"She is a single mast sloop, able to carry thirty-five tons of cargo."

"What type of cargo did she carry?"

"Rum, timber, textiles, molasses, sugar…" I paused, to give him time to write.

"No armaments, correct?"

"Correct."

"The advertisement said twenty-two hundred," he said, staring intently.

"That is the price."

"How far is the wharf?" he asked, closing his pocketbook and getting up out of his seat.

"It is within walking distance. Not too far."

"Show me the way."

With growing urgency, I walked toward the wharf. A myriad of vessels, ships, brigs, schooners, and sloops, dotted the bustling docks. Sailors and crewmen scattered among them, the clamor of repairs and the cacophony of shouted orders adding to my already anxious mind. And there, in a rare state of stillness, the *Friendship* rested in her berth, her ropes murmuring like soft, mournful sighs, her sails tucked away in a semblance of repose.

We quickly made it onto the sloop. I guided Mr. Williams on a tour of the vessel, attempting to highlight all her best features, from the well-caulked hull to her sleek and sharp bow to the sturdy single mast with well-organized rigging. When we were finished, I stood on the deck for a long, contemplative moment, my hands resting on the warm railing.

"There is a bit of upkeep to be had and upgrades to make to get her in the shape I need. The cabin is quite small for one. And I noticed loose planks near the port side and…"

"We are willing to negotiate," I interjected.

"I can offer sixteen hundred, and I will pay right now, in silver."

My heart sank with disappointment. That was well below the lowest price.

"Would you be willing to pay nineteen hundred?"

He shook his head intently. "I know that this is a family ship, and there may be some sentimental value. But sentimental value is meaningless. Seventeen hundred is the best I can do. I am sure this is the best offer you will get, given the condition and age. Unless you want the ship to continue to linger and others catch wind it couldn't sell?"

I contemplated his words long and hard. I had clear instructions to not sell below nineteen hundred dollars. But he made a strong pitch.

"I will need an answer. This is the best opportunity you will have."

I took a deep breath and looked at him intently. "You have a deal. We can finalize the contract in the counting house here in the wharf."

"Excellent."

I escorted Mr. Williams to the counting house where we finalized the sale. Though we were parting from Father's first vessel, we were now more financially secure, able to sustain our needs for the near future. As I headed home, with the silver coins in a bag, I anticipated how relieved my mother would be.

When I arrived, I hurried through the front door and entered her room, where she and my two sisters were mending clothes.

"Did you make contact with Mr. Williams?"

"Yes, I did," handing her the bag of money.

"Well, how did it go?"

"It went well. Though he was a bit of a shrewd negotiator."

My mother's countenance immediately lifted. "How much did you settle on?"

"Seventeen hundred."

She paused, staring at me with wide eyes. "I told you no lower than nineteen hundred," she shouted, throwing the clothes to the floor.

"I know. But he pointed out its age and the work that was needed," I replied, frustration building within me.

"You should have come to me before you decided on this."

"Mother, I am sorry."

"Did you finalize the paperwork?"

"Yes. He said he had to leave in a hurry."

"I am in utter disbelief," she exclaimed.

"You were the one who wanted to sell the ship!"

My mother rose up out of her chair, shaking her head. My sisters had stopped mending the clothes, staring at me with blank faces. As my mother left the room, she said under her breath, "Just like you sold the books your father got for you."

"What did you say?!" I replied, heading back towards her.

"You sold your books! Probably for a low price as well. You don't seem to see the value in the things associated with your father."

"That's not true. I…" I had nothing else to say as I stood in the hallway, perplexed and void of confidence. I never wanted the responsibility in the first place. Yet in that fleeting opportunity, I was reminded why I had avoided being involved in the family business. Whatever I did, it was always found wanting.

Chapter 14 (August) – A Soirée

Soon after we sold my father's sloop, I found myself in the familiar comforts of the Green Dragon Tavern. For a moment, I considered the gaming tables below. The lure of the card games—where I'd had better luck than at hazard—tempted me to join. But I shook the thought away. Instead, I ordered a pint and took a seat in the corner, alone to contemplate my missteps. The first pint vanished too quickly, the bitter tang doing little to quiet the storm in my mind. A second pint did little to settle me either. Something deeper ate at me, something no amount of ale could silence.

I was still wading through the murky fog of confusion from the sale of my father's ship, only to find Owen entering. He spotted me from afar, then walked towards me in his usual friendly manner. When he arrived at my table, his gaze swept over me with the practiced precision of a tailor determining whether a sleeve had been cut a quarter-inch too short.

"Something bothering you, Caleb?"

"No, nothing at all," I replied, tipping the tankard to my mouth.

"I know you too well, my friend. Something is not right."

"We sold the *Friendship*."

"Your father's first ship? Why? What happened?"

"We had to. I don't know. I'm confused. I sold it for less than what we wanted. We weren't going to utilize it. So I made a deal."

"Well, did your mother agree on the final price?"

"No. Though she wanted to sell it in the first place."

"You should have at least consulted her first."

I took another long drink. Maybe he was right. But perhaps it would all quiet down and be forgotten before long.

"Are you having a pint?"

"Just one. I can't hang around tonight. I need to be up early. It's been long hours this past week."

Owen sipped his ale while I took down the last of mine and ordered another.

"My cousin Catherine is hosting a gathering on Saturday. You should come," Owen said, his gleeful countenance beginning to irk my nerves.

"If it's a tea party, I kindly decline."

"It's a soirée. Dancing, dinner, games, and punch." He smirked.

"Count me out."

"Maryann will be there."

I scoffed. "She already has a suitor who outclasses me."

"Charles won't be attending," Owen said in a conspiratorial tone.

I folded my arms. "How do you know?"

"My mother is friendly with Mrs. Hayes. I overheard their talk. Charles is going hunting with Mr. Hayes this weekend. Apparently, it's considered quite the milestone."

I took another long drink, considering. "Hmm…well, if that's the case, my odds might improve. Though it's just one evening."

Owen clapped a hand on my shoulder. "At the very least, it will be a distraction."

"You are too kind, my friend," I said with a smile.

Owen finished his pint of ale, then soon after, got up from the table, and left. He was always there for me, in times of joy and times in pain. After he left, I set my half-full tankard down and departed, wondering if just possibly I might be able to connect with Maryann in a more meaningful way.

The days leading up to the soirée passed like a ship marooned at sea. One moment, I resolved to go; the next, I questioned the wisdom of it. I pictured the evening unfolding, imagining my presence amid the town's finest. Yet, the chance of seeing Maryann and admittedly, of meeting those who might aid my inquiries into the indigo transaction, proved irresistible.

On the afternoon of the gathering, I donned formal stockings and a pressed linen shirt, but the finery felt borrowed and flashy. One look in the mirror and my confidence melted. So, I threw off the ridiculous clothes, pulled on a pair of breeches, a cotton shirt, and a blue vest with the top button unfastened, and set out for the gathering at Catherine's house towards Bowdoin Square.

I weaved through crowded streets full of cunning merchants and busy townspeople. Past the stalls filled with fish, carts full of produce, and loud vendors soliciting business until I reached Court

Street. I passed by printing shops, offices, and other storefronts until I reached Bowdoin Square. Before me was a mix of old-fashioned wooden homes and new, grander federal-style townhouses lining the road, with tall, symmetrically aligned white windows and brick facades. Yet, the Williams' house stood out, rising three stories high, its refined federal-style façade towered above its neighbors, with five perfectly placed windows lining each floor. I immediately felt out of place as I spotted a couple exit their carriage, dressed for an elegant occasion. My pulse rapidly sped up, but luckily, Owen was waiting outside, his familiar grin easing my nerves.

"You made it!" he said, his arms wide open as though he had never seen me before.

I smirked. "Had you not called out, I might not have recognized you in that coat."

Owen glanced down at his tailored attire. "Yes, yes, laugh it up. And you? Shedding all pomp and circumstance, I see."

We stepped inside, where a servant greeted us warmly. "Hello, Mr. Owen. Who is your companion?"

"Caleb Thompson, a good friend of mine."

The servant bowed slightly. "Welcome to the Williams' house, sir. Coffee is being served in the parlor. Dinner shall follow, with music and dancing later in the evening."

The ceilings were intricately decorated with molding wrapped around its edges. Each painting that lined the walls was framed in gold. The aroma of lavender and candle wax wafted in the air, a stark contrast to the salt and tar of the harbor. Owen and I entered the parlor and grabbed some coffee. The fine porcelain cup felt fragile in my hands, slightly shifting as I took a sip. We stood there at the room's edge, observing guests as they arrived. Owen's cousin, Catherine, soon swept in, flanked by her friends, their silk gowns glinting in the sunlight. But my attention barely lingered since Maryann was not among them. Catherine greeted Owen with the ease of familiarity.

"Hello, cousin. And this is… Caleb, am I right?" she said, turning to me.

I bowed slightly. "A pleasure."

"No Maryann tonight?" Owen asked, knowing full well she was on my mind.

Catherine shook her head. "She said she'd come, but who knows? Why are my friends not to your liking?" she teased.

Before Owen could form a reply, Catherine and her friends left, continuing with another conversation, their laughter trailing them. I began to doubt why I would stick around, given Maryann was not there. Though I was with Owen, my restlessness grew as I imagined the evening carrying on with conversations that felt rehearsed and the formality, suffocating.

While Owen managed to keep my company for a few more moments, I grew unattached, noticing a small group of prominent-looking business men gathered near the back of the parlor. One wore a crimson waistcoat beneath his black tailcoat, while another adorned a red handkerchief prominently displayed in his pocket. Amidst the group was a young man who looked quite familiar. His black frock coat and appearance was one I recognized from church, the young man who was talking to Mr. Hayes.

While I schemed on how to learn more about the men, movement near the hallway caught my eye. Maryann had arrived.

She moved with her quiet grace, her pretty red hair in a ponytail to her right. She wore an indigo gown, its deep hue complementing her beauty. A row of small buttons fastened the bodice beneath her bust, accentuating a high waistline. The sleeves ended short on her shoulder, leaving her arms bare, while a modestly white-lined neckline traced her neck. She was by far the most beautiful one there.

Owen nudged me. "I told you she would be here," he murmured.

Catherine came to greet Maryann as she walked towards the parlor.

"I am sorry I am late. I had to complete my studies before I came," Maryann said graciously.

"Don't worry about it. Just in time for dinner," Catherine said as her friends joined to greet Maryann.

"If Charles were here, he would be gushing right now," one of the girls said.

Maryann laughed, waving off the young woman. She was right. And I couldn't have stuck out more in the opposite of ways. Maryann glanced over. Her countenance brightened even more. I nodded. Maybe she was just being nice. Or maybe she was happy to see me there.

Dinner was served, and the guests filled in their seats. Maryann was at the far end of the table, where I could see her captivating beauty, while I sat next to the group of men I had noticed earlier with Owen also next to me. I turned to the man with the red handkerchief.

"Hello, my name is Caleb Thompson," I said, holding out a shaky hand.

"Elias Hathway," he replied, keeping his grip strong while studying me. "Thompson…ah yes, I knew I recognized that name. Your father owns the Atlantic Shipping Co., am I right?"

"That is correct. Forgive me for intruding."

Then the young man with the black frock coat cordially introduced himself. "I'm Dameron Payne."

I nodded. He appeared in his thirties and was certainly the youngest of the group. He had a certain charm about him, one that was not pretentious like the others.

"Mr. Thompson, I believe we have met before. Gideon Carter," the man with the red waistcoat said.

"Yes, I believe we have. Nice to see you," I said, trying to recall when I had met him.

"You were explaining how the fur trade was faring," Mr. Payne said, looking at Mr. Carter.

"Well, it's risky and quite lengthy. If you can make it around Cape Horn without shipwreck, then you improve your chances. If you get to the Northwest Coast and club enough seals…well, and don't encounter violent locals, your odds improve slightly more. Yet you will also have to dodge pirates, disease, and perilous weather as you travel months to Canton, where chances improve significantly more."

The men jeered in unison. I could only slightly snicker, as it all seemed too pretentious to me.

"To answer your question, it is lucrative but dangerous. Perhaps I should have gone the route you have taken through the Standard Shipping Co. and went straight from Boston to China," Mr. Carter said, looking back at Mr. Payne.

"Perhaps, but I prefer to have fewer competitors than many," Mr. Payne replied.

The men had more laughs, then drank their madeira wine.

"Caleb, what are your stances on the war between Napoleon and Britain?" Mr. Hathaway asked, shifting to a more serious conversation.

I immediately regretted ever introducing myself. I struggled for an answer for such a lofty question.

"Well, the British are overstepping their boundaries if you ask me."

"As you know, many in Boston favor Britain, given our economic ties and their dominance of the sea," Mr. Carter explained.

"Or oppose Napolean…" added Mr. Hathaway.

"Give the young man a break. His father was conscripted by the Royal Navy," Mr. Payne interjected.

"Well, if I can give you any advice, don't hold such narrow views. Try to broaden your viewpoint beyond the circumstances of your father. Boston is becoming the trade hub of the New World," Mr. Hathaway declared.

I felt my anger rise at once. Narrow view? He was the narrow-minded one, focused solely on wealth.

"Yes," Mr. Carter countered, "but if we fail to align ourselves in this war, we risk making enemies of both Napoleon and Britain."

"We should side with Britain. Their naval strength is unrivaled, and Napoleon is a tyrannical usurper," Mr. Hathaway said, raising a glass. "To our enduring freedom."

As I listened to their ostentatious chatter, I felt smaller and smaller. All their pomp and pretense made me feel inferior. However, during the conversation, I gained a good understanding of each of their backgrounds: Mr. Hathaway dealt in sugar and textiles, while Mr. Carter was the owner of a fur trading business that took a long route from Boston to the Northwest Coast to China, and Mr. Payne imported Chinese goods through the Standard Shipping Co., owned by Mr. Hayes. My interest waned when I learned Mr. Carter, the man with the red handkerchief, had spent most of the year abroad. Clearly, none had any dealing with indigo. Even more frustrating, there was no clarity of what came after "red—" in my father's journal. Red what? My mind became overwhelmed as I calculated through endless possibilities.

Eventually, the dining table was cleared while guests filed to the parlor, where the ceilings pitched high. Musicians struck up a tune, joined by a harpsichord, violinist, and flutist, with couples forming lines for a dance, women on one side and men on the other. As Maryann remained unpaired, my heart pounded as I saw my opportunity. With a deep breath, I stepped over to line up with her, nearly stumbling in my haste.

Next to me was Owen. He leaned in. "Ever danced before?"

"Never," I admitted.

"Just don't trip."

As the music struck up, each couple took hands and moved down the middle of the set, weaving back into their places in rhythm with the tune. Then came our turn. I approached Maryann and took her hand, the warmth of her touch steadying me. Our eyes locked as though we were the only ones in the room; then a slow smile formed on her lips.

"Caleb, so good to see you here."

"I'm glad you arrived," I said with a bright smile. I was having an uninterrupted moment with her and it filled me with great happiness.

Together, we went down through the set, each step in harmony, and soon returned to stand in our place. Shockingly, I managed not to fall. By the dance's end, my nerves had settled, replaced by exhilaration. The music continued while some of the guests continued to dance, while others separated into groups by age and familiarity.

Owen, myself, and a few of the fellows, made our way into the parlor for cards, joined by some of the young women. The older company kept apart, while we gathered for our own merriment. Shortly after, Catherine brought out some rum punch and set it on the table. While we played a few hands, I noticed Maryann standing next to the door, apparently ready to leave. I listened into the conversation as Catherine approached her.

"Thank you, Catherine, I've had a lovely time. But I must return now, for my father needs my help with a few matters."

"Is this about your father's business or what Charles might think?"

I quickly put my cards down and walked up to them, waiting for Catherine to finish. Then, without hesitation, I found myself confessing a little too much. "Your company has been the highlight of my evening. Might I persuade you to stay just a little longer?"

She hesitated, peering over at the table and back at me.

"It's good to take a break from the demands of everyday life. Join us for some card games."

Maryann smiled. "I suppose I could stay a bit longer," she said, her eyes fixed on mine.

"What game do you prefer?"

"I do enjoy whist."

The evening stretched on with laughter filling the room and friendship building amongst us. We played some whist, then some loo, enjoying rum punch and levity. After a few hours, Catherine announced it was time for her to retire for the night. The remaining guests lined up and exited the house, the spirit of elation and fellowship filling each one's heart. When I stepped out into the warm summer night, I found that it was not the grandeur of the estate or the finery of the guests that lingered in my mind. Rather, it was the quiet thrill of Maryann's laughter, the echo of her voice in the candlelit parlor, and the possibility of something more that kept me reminiscing.

Chapter 15 (August) – A Hopeful Scoop

After the soirée, I became more motivated to work hard than ever before. Not because I was being forced to, but because I wanted a place in Maryann's world. And to be able to be in her world, I would have to earn it. The following week, I worked tirelessly in the counting room, meticulously entering into the ledger, reviewing contracts, and ensuring debts that were due were paid. One day, Owen arrived at the counting room, his presence a quiet joy. He slapped his hand on the desk, his grin as easy as ever.

"Working hard these days, are you?" he teased, eyeing the ledger in front of me.

"Well, if I want to make any impression on Maryann, I will need to," I admitted.

I waited anxiously, hoping for him to mention his cousin's gathering, or more importantly, if he had heard anything from Maryann. But he said nothing. With each passing moment, my patience thinned.

"I'm glad I went to your cousin's," I ventured. "It was a great time."

Yet he gave me no inkling. Owen just shrugged. "It was fine, I suppose," he said, walking towards the window.

That was it? Just fine? Had that night with Maryann been nothing more than a passing amusement? Had I misunderstood everything? I was about to let the topic drop when Owen's expression shifted. A suggestive smirk curled at the edge of his mouth as he leaned in.

"I know what you want to hear."

"Do you?"

"Oh, I don't know. Let's not let romance ruin a perfectly good day." He paused, letting the moment stretch.

"Well, if you have nothing to say, why bring it up at all?"

Owen laughed, then finally broke his silence. "Friend, I think you have a chance with Maryann."

The words caught me off guard. I blinked hard, unsure if I had misheard him. "You aren't playing a cruel joke on me are you?" I inquired.

"She was talking about you to my cousin."

I sat forward, my fingers curling around a quill pen. "She was?"

"Said you were fun to be around. That you have admirable qualities."

"Admirable qualities?"

"Carefree," he clarified. Then, with a sly look, he added, "She also mentioned you had nice dark hair and exquisite blue eyes."

I dropped the quill pen and leaned back, letting the words settle over me like the warmth from the sun on a summer afternoon. I had thought of Maryann constantly since that night, but now, for the first time, I had something more than my own hopeful intuition. I made a positive impression on her!

Owen watched me, amused. "Well? What are you thinking?"

I exhaled, steadying my voice. "I think I should call on her. But…"

"But what?"

"We just sold one of our ships, and…"

"She obviously seems to have interest in you, the person, not your family's status." He looked at me intently. "I can help you write a note to her family. You'll need their permission first. If they agree, she'll respond."

It was an offer I hadn't considered, but before I could thank him, Owen's tone slightly changed.

"But don't forget," he added, "Charles is still courting her."

A sudden weight bore down on my shoulders. For a moment, I had pushed Charles to the back of my mind.

"What do you know about him?" I asked, my stomach tightening.

Owen brushed his chin with his hand, his expression thoughtful. "Other than the fact that he's wealthy, thanks to his father's wealth?! He's cunning in business, of course. A superb hunter. Is quite acquainted with the subject of history. And, of course, the Hayes family likes him."

He paused, then added, "And, well…you've seen him. Handsome enough to turn heads."

A bitter laugh escaped me. "I understand," I said, my voice sharper than I intended. "He's better than me."

Owen shook his head. "That's not what I'm saying. Look, I have to go. But I wanted to pass this along."

"Thanks, friend. Have the most splendid of days."

Owen left but the thought of my inferiority had already settled, burrowing into that part of me that was always keenly aware of my shortcomings. I finished the final entry into the ledger and set the pen down with a dull thud. With all of Charles's superior qualities, he also appeared to be the type of person who won. Every time. I pictured the night I got into deep debt and the man who convinced me to play hazard and ultimately took me for all the money I had. But I had not forgotten that I did dig myself out of that hole. The feelings of inadequacy slowly diminished, and I began to feel deep, unrelenting determination. Charles or not, I would not let him dictate my actions. I had never felt this way about a woman before, and now, I had a reason to compete for her. Maryann had thought of me, and that was enough to carry me forward.

Chapter 16 (August) – Courting Above One's Station

The next morning, I dressed with deliberate care. My dark blue waistcoat was freshly pressed, breeches immaculate, and boots polished to a subtle gleam. The notion of drafting a formal note to Maryann's family seemed unnecessary. It didn't make sense to entangle myself in the delays of correspondence when I could secure an answer in person.

Stepping onto Beacon Street, the significance of my intentions settled over me. I continued, though I wavered with thoughts of being rejected. When the Hayes residence came into view, perched on the gentle slope on Beacon Hill, it was more imposing than I had imagined. Similar to the Federal-style homes nearby, yet enormous in its size, their residence was the left side of mirroring adjoined townhomes. Their residence overlooked the Common, with three bays wide and four stories high stretching towards the clouds. The adjoined dwellings consisted of twenty-four tall windows, each with white shutters and decorative moulding, set evenly upon the brick facade.

With each step, my confidence dwindled as I got closer to the house. I wondered if the Hayes family would even grant me an audience. My name carried no great fortune, no notable lineage.

Charles Derby, by contrast, was wealth and refinement personified. My heart gripped my chest, with doubts flooding in. But then, I recalled Maryann's laughter at the dance and the way her gaze lingered just a moment longer than necessary. That memory propelled me forward as I climbed the steps to their front door. I lifted the brass knocker and rapped it firmly. The sound resounded: clack, clack, clack. There was no turning back now. Moments later, the door opened to reveal the family servant standing with a short coat and standing collar, his expression stoic.

"Good morning," I said, half-confidently. "I've come to call on Miss Maryann Hayes."

The servant looked at me up and down briefly, glancing as though he was weighing my character more than my appearance. A crawl of discomfort ran through me at the thought of his judgment.

"Your name, young man?"

"Caleb Thompson."

He paused while uncomfortably continuing to look at me before he said, "Wait here."

I stood on the brick steps, the fanlight above the door casting fractured patterns of light across my chest. From within, muffled voices drifted through an open window.

"Who?" came a sharp inquiry from another man whom I suspected was Mr. Hayes.

"A Mr. Caleb Thompson."

"If it's who I think it is, I don't approve. He is no gentleman… He consumes strong spirits and gambles," said the man who must have been Mr. Hayes.

His words crushed my spirit. I instantly regretted ever coming, as what I feared was developing right before me.

"This may be an opportunity," came another clipped remark, from a softer, feminine voice who I suspected was Mrs. Hayes.

A muffled argument began unfolding between them, her tone carrying a note of persuasion.

An opportunity for what?

The voices faded, and then a few moments later, footsteps approached. The wooden door opened, and to my surprise, the servant greeted me with a slight grin.

"Please, come in. I am Mr. Boyle, by the way."

"Nice to meet you, sir."

I stepped inside the Hayes residence, careful with my steps, the polished wood floors gleaming beneath my feet, a crystal chandelier overhead, its facets glistening in the light. Gilded mirrors reflected every refined detail of the interior. Mr. Boyle escorted me up a flight of stairs. Above me were continuous stairs winding towards the fourth floor. The grandeur and refinement of their residence made me deeply inadequate. Then he led me to the parlor.

"Please, have a seat. Miss Maryann will be down shortly."

In the room, richly upholstered furniture encircled a marble fireplace, the air carrying the warm scent of beeswax and of parchment from old books. I took a seat in an ornate wooden chair, willing my nerves to steady. The walls were lined with fine paintings, the shelves filled with books that had likely been imported at great expense. This was their world, a world where I was a clear outcast. As I waited, I fought the urge to stand, to pace.

Moments later, Mr. Hayes entered the room. His expression was polite yet composed.

"Good morning, Mr. Thompson," he greeted.

"Good morning, Mr. Hayes. It's a pleasure to meet you," I said, anxiously rising from the chair.

Waving his hand, he gestured for me to remain seated as he took a chair opposite mine. He raised his chin and took a long look at me. "Please understand, as a father, I am in the business of knowing who my daughter keeps company with. How did you become acquainted with Maryann?"

"We have mutual friends. But the first time we met was at the bookstore," I managed to explain.

His brow lifted slightly. "Do you read?"

"Not as often as I once did," I responded, wanting the words to be forgotten as they left my mouth.

"I see." Mr. Hayes looked away and paused.

I could see his thoughts wandering, towards doubt, I assumed. So, I continued, "We were both recently at her friend Catherine's gathering."

He pondered more. "Yes, she came home late that night."

As he said those words, I became even more anxious. I struggled to find a positive jumping off point. "We also had spent some time at the Fourth of July celebration."

"I don't recall seeing you around."

"It was a large crowd, sir."

"Indeed." His gaze held more skepticism now. "Do you work for your father's business?"

"Yes, sir. It carries great responsibility," I said, knowing that I was just a novice to the industry and nowhere near his level of experience.

"A man can make a decent living in this business," Mr. Hayes mused, rubbing his jaw. "But fortune, I've learned, favors those with patience, persistence, and good ethics."

"I wholeheartedly agree," I replied, hoping the conversation would finally turn in my favor.

"I don't mean to pry, but tell me about your father's conscription."

I cleared my throat. "Well, he was taken quite abruptly, singled out, I would say… It has been extremely difficult to understand."

"Singled out? It must feel that way, I suppose. St. Kitts was where this took place, am I right?"

"Yes, St. Kitts," I said, recalling how heavy the news was the day I heard it.

Before he could inquire further, footsteps in the hallway interrupted us. Then Maryann appeared in the doorway.

"Father, could you stop interrogating Caleb?"

"Oh…we were having a pleasant conversation…right, Mr. Thompson?" he replied, looking at me.

"Of course, very pleasant," I responded, looking back at Maryann.

Mr. Hayes chuckled. "I'll leave you two to your conversation."

With that, he departed, and the tension in my body immediately released.

Maryann turned to me, her deep green eyes captivating all my attention. "It's good to see you, Caleb."

"The feeling is mutual," I said, my nerves softening under her friendly smile. "Your home is wonderful."

"It was designed by a prominent architect. It is an exact mirror of the adjoining home, except for one feature that I am proud of."

"What would that be?"

"My garden. Let me show you."

Maryann led me outside to the garden in the back, where a narrow walled off yard with a gravel pathway wove with more flowers than I could keep track: vibrant clusters of tulips of various colors, pink peonies, and white and red roses. The scent of summer blossoms filled the air.

"This must have taken years to cultivate," I remarked.

"It has," she said, surveying with quiet pride. "Each season I add something new."

"It's lovely." Her affinity for the garden made me admire her more. It fit her authenticity and in a way, an extension of her inner beauty, calm, compassionate.

She smiled at me, and in that moment, I was completely immersed in her presence.

"I had a great time at Catherine's home," I said in an attempt to rekindle the bond we had that evening.

"I must admit, that was one of the most remarkable gatherings I've attended. I do wish I could enjoy such moments more often."

Her words startled me. Maryann, who surely attended the finest gatherings, counted this among her favorites! With that, I resolved all the more firmly.

"Ledgers, shipments, contracts…it's all so…suffocating."

"Well, yes, it can be. But it's also your family's livelihood in your case, isn't it?"

"Of course. I do not wish to be bound by it." I stopped talking, realizing what I was uttering was not quite the approach a young man would take if he wanted to impress a young woman. Especially for someone with her status. So, I changed the subject.

"Did you happen to pick up *The Mysteries of Udolpho* from the bookstore that day?"

"I did!"

"What do you think?"

"I confess I lost sleep over those secret passages and old castles! And the heroine, she was complex in her nature, obedient, filled with virtue but a bit too sentimental."

"Very nice analysis."

We continued our conversation, our rapport deepening as we sat and enjoyed the open summer air. She spoke of social gatherings and the expectations placed upon her as a young woman. I listened, absorbing every word, every inflection. But the time passed too quickly, and when Mr. Boyle appeared to summon her for lunch, I quickly scrambled for another moment together.

"Might I have the pleasure of seeing you again?"

She met my eyes, and without hesitation, she said, "Absolutely."

"A walk, perhaps?"

Her smile deepened. "That would be perfect. There are quite exquisite views from here."

"Does next Tuesday work for you?"

"Yes, indeed it does."

As I departed the Hayes residence, Mr. Payne and a young woman were entering a carriage outside of the adjoined townhouse. He greeted me, and I went along my way, the afternoon sun illuminating the cobblestones of Beacon Street. Something unfamiliar stirred within me. Hope. Perhaps fortune, at last, was beginning to turn in my favor.

Chapter 17 (September) – Stroll Along the Slopes of Beacon Hill

Maryann and I met the next week for a late morning stroll along the slopes of Beacon Hill. She wore a white shawl draped over her shoulders, the soft fabric catching in the breeze. Everything she did, she did with ease. As for myself, I was nervous. More than I cared to admit. And yet, I could not help but feel a quiet thrill, for I was walking with her. Only a short time ago, such a moment would have been beyond my reach.

We made our way along the well-worn pathways towards the summit of the hill. It was one of those days that will forever be etched in my memory. The trees of the Common still held their green, though hints of gold and russet had begun to show, whispering of the autumn soon to come. As we continued, a brilliant red cardinal swooped by and landed on a branch, then landed on another branch, calling out in its familiar repetitive call.

Many townspeople gathered to take in the beautiful scenery that day. Maryann waved to a man she knew, and it was obvious he was surprised to see her with someone other than Charles. The cool morning air was laced with the distant hum of the harbor and the murmur of the lively town. Eastward, across Boston Harbor, merchant ships and fishing vessels arrived and departed from the docks. We could even make out the islands dotting the bay. To the West, the Charles River with its wide, glistening expanse shimmered under the sunlight. Across the river was Charlestown lined with its wooden houses, wharves, and shipyards. Southward we could see Boston's winding streets, colonial homes, churches, and marketplaces gradually thickening toward the town center.

"The views from here say it all about the town," she mused.

"It does quite well. You are fortunate to live nearby. I can imagine the views from your home."

"They are quite exquisite. We have a water view from the fourth floor. And a view of the Common from the front."

"Does Mr. Payne own the adjoining townhome?"

"He leases from my father."

"Ah, I see. I saw him when I was leaving your home the other day. He was with a young woman."

"Oh yes, Brigid. He has been courting her for about six months now. Many wonder where it's all going."

"Does your father do a lot of business with him?"

"Yes, he is one of my father's largest clients."

"In the China trade, am I right?"

"Yes, he sells goods from China that my father imports for him, of course. According to my father, his business has grown quite significantly over recent years. He began doing business with my father some years back. That's how my father and he met. Then he moved in next door when we finished the construction of our home."

I see," I said quietly. We continued our walk, the sun warm upon us and the views before us splendid. "I am glad for this time together."

"The sentiment is mutual. Plus, I needed a break from the monotony."

"You are beginning to sound like me!"

Maryann let out a long laugh. "Well, maybe I agree with you…to a certain extent."

We paused for a while, watching the ships in the harbor below.

"Do you see yourself staying here in Boston all your life?"

She looked at me curiously. "I love it here, if you haven't already noticed. But I do have to say…"

I looked at her, hoping she was not becoming uncomfortable.

"I am sorry. I have to say that with all the pressures to marry, it is difficult to think too far into the future."

"I can imagine. Please take no offense. But if you were to have the perfect suitor, what would he be?"

Her cheeks turned deep red.

"I apologize. I didn't mean to…"

"No, it's quite fine. I wouldn't want him to be perfect. Perfect means dishonesty. I would want honesty, authenticity, and someone who understood me, of course. Someone I could laugh with. Rather than always being forced to be proper for."

"Hmmm…I am surprised."

Her expression turned wry. "Why do you say that?"

"Well, I mean, Charles seems to have everything."

She tilted her head at me. "And you? What does your future look like? I imagine your share of responsibilities has been difficult as of late."

"It's a great deal all at once," I admitted. "With my father gone, the weight of our business falls squarely on me and the competition is…nothing short of relentless."

She offered a smile. "I understand. My father's business is demanding. I'm not directly involved, but I do get dragged into it from time to time."

We carried on, and by this point, I began sharing everything I knew about my father's business. I spoke openly, perhaps more openly than I should have. Part of me wanted to avoid the topic altogether; it only reminded me of his absence and the heavy burden of keeping things afloat. But I wished to impress her, to assure her I was no idle sort. She listened intently, her questions thoughtful, her quiet presence reassuring.

After some time, we continued with other subjects, from her plans for her garden to her desire to go to the theater one day. We walked along the promenade of developing federal-style townhouses till our walk came to a well-measured ending. Then, just like that, she departed in her carriage, leaving me with the lingering warmth of her company. Though I was uncertain if I could keep up with the standards of her position in society, I hoped I could see her again.

Chapter 18 (September) – Dissent

Though my courtship with Maryann had been progressing, life, as most would know, is seldom a straight wake upon calm seas. While in the parlor one late September afternoon, I found myself subjected to familiar parental scrutiny.

"Could I have a word with you?" my mother asked, her words already causing me foreboding.

"Of course, what is it?"

With her arms crossed, she locked her focus on me, leaving me with no escape. "Charlotte mentioned you've taken a romantic interest in someone?"

I sighed. Though I wished it never would, this was a conversation that would inevitably have taken place. I tamped down my irritation before responding.

"There's no need to make a great deal of it."

Arching an eyebrow, she said, "I heard you went to her home."

"Yes…and it went well. In fact, we had a nice walk together as well."

"Caleb, Maryann is a fine young woman, but…"

“Go on.”

“Well, you do not suit her disposition.”

Her words landed with a sting. She wasn't wrong.

“I don’t think you understand. When we interact, it's real.”

“Son, I just don’t think her father will let you get too close to her in the end.”

“But he has not objected to us seeing each other yet.”

“I hope you won’t take this amiss, but have you reflected on where your loyalty lies of late?”

“My loyalty? Must we revisit this again? Always the same criticism, the same fault-finding.”

"You forgot! Her father owns a shipping company that’s expanding to the West Indies..."

“You should have spared me the other words and come straight to the point.”

I remained quiet. She was wrong. She wasn’t there when Maryann and I were together. If she had been, maybe she too would have seen the bond we had. But maybe it was her experience in life or the confidence behind her words that made me less sure about where this was all going. She exhaled, letting the matter rest, then changed the subject.

"You need to check with Liam about the departure of *Eleanor*. He mentioned there’s an issue with the provisions."

With my escape presented to me, I did not hesitate. I left the house at once, heading to the wharf as the sun began its descent. I wondered what my mother meant by the phrase ‘an issue with the provisions'. With matters influx we made recent changes and it was beginning to get difficult to track. In my father's absence, Liam was promoted to captain of *Eleanor*, while *Providence* came under the command of Captain Eldridge, who had previously served aboard *Eleanor*. *Eleanor* still lay anchored in the harbor, though by now, it should have been gone.

"Caleb," he barked, his voice tight with frustration. "Who did you consult when ordering these provisions?"

"I based it on previous voyages."

"So you didn't talk to the first mate about this or anyone else who might know better?"

"No, I didn't," I admitted.

"Every voyage is different. Luckily, I caught this; otherwise, we would have run out of provisions, and the men would have been very disconcerted, to say the least."

Embarrassment flared hot in my face.

"Nothing new from him!" a crewman quipped, his tone laced with amusement.

Liam shot him a glare. "Shut it, you landlubber. If you've got nothing useful to say, keep your mouth shut."

Turning back to me, he added, "Where's your head, son? You need to fix this. Now!"

I forced a nod, my stomach coiling under the tension. "I'll make it right. I'll go to the market in the morning."

"Yes, good thought. But first, you need to make sense of this mess. Count the provisions tonight."

"Tonight?"

“Yes, tonight,” he said, the veins in his neck protruding. Liam, though tough as they come, was usually composed. But assuredly, the pressure to maintain a well-run ship was getting to him, and I was right in the middle of it.

“Have I stayed with your father’s business up until this point?”

“Yes, and it is appreciated.”

“And you know I have a family to provide for.”

“Yes, of course.”

“I don’t think you quite understand, lad. Listen to me carefully. If the company can’t sustain, then I don’t know if I can as well. And I am sure the men feel the same way. Hear me?”

“Yes, I understand.”

Liam walked away, cursing intensely while I stayed behind feeling the urge to grab a drink at the tavern. The pressure was beginning to get to me. As the docks fell silent for the evening, I stayed aboard, rifling through the casks of dried fish, the barrels of salted beef, and the endless stores of rice, flour, beer, cider, and rum. Eventually, the once-busy wharf emptied, save for a few lingering souls. Ironically, the last time I’d been aboard this ship, my father had scolded me for knocking over a stack of cargo. The memory, long buried, emerged like a ghost—unnerving and unwelcome. I could still feel the sting of that moment: the urge to run, the burden of shame dragging my confidence.

As I worked through the remaining provisions, I noticed a peculiar interaction on a vessel owned by Bellamy Trading Co. There, on the deck, stood John Lowe and beside him, a customs officer. That in itself wasn't unusual. But what was strange was the exchange. A small bag passed from John's hands to the officer's. The customs officer glanced around, then pocketed it with a nod. Customs duties were paid in the office, not in the dim corners of a ship's deck. Furthermore, there was no apparent reason for a payment since there was no cargo being unloaded. When the customs officer's gaze swept over the docks and landed on me, my body became rigid. Then, I slowly went back to counting the provisions, acting as if I had not witnessed a thing. Within a few short moments, the customs officer turned on his heel, descended from the ship, and disappeared down the dock with the look of a man who did not wish to be followed. Then John Lowe appeared in the distant view and looked my way, watching my every movement. I continued to count the inventory, wondering what had transpired. Maybe it was nothing. But slowly, a quiet unease crept into my bones. I had no proof of wrongdoing, only the certainty I had seen something I was not meant to. After hours of counting, reassessing what we had and what was needed, I left the dock with my focus on leaving without being confronted about what I witnessed.

Early the next morning, I swiftly made my way to the market. Though I was able to secure more provisions, there would be a significant delay to the departure of *Eleanor*. When I informed Liam, I braced for his inevitable scorn. But there was none, and somehow that was worse. His silent anger made me think this might be his last voyage with the Atlantic Shipping Co.

Chapter 19 (October) – Competition Closes In

When the final preparations for *Eleanor's* departure were complete, I stood at the docks, watching as the ship slipped beyond the horizon. A sense of relief settled over me, but only momentarily. I had a new challenge to think about. As I made my way to the counting room, my thoughts drifted to Maryann. I contemplated how I might see her again and whether she had thought of me since our last meeting. But when I arrived at the counting house, before I even opened the door, my musing was abruptly shattered by the sharp urgency of my mother's voice.

"Caleb, I bring you ill news," she said, stepping into the room.

I instantly became unsettled by the gravity in her expression.

"Several accounts have severed their contracts with us," she said.

"Why, what happened?"

"The Standard Shipping Co. has cut their rates for West Indies routes," she said, fixing an accusing stare upon me.

Her words landed harshly. I knew what would follow. Before she could say another word, I intervened.

"I know exactly what you want to say. But this has nothing to do with Maryann."

"Were I not concerned, Caleb, I would hold my tongue. But I am, and I would not see you come to be harmed by her."

"I've had enough talking about this matter with you!"

My mother did not respond with her words. Instead, she handed me a folded note. I unfolded it, the scent of fresh ink curling into the air. The message was brief, but its implications unmistakable:

The Thompson family has no place here. Sell your business and depart Boston at once!

My grip on the paper tightened. "Where did this come from?" I demanded, anger filling my voice.

"I found it under the front door of the house after you left," she replied.

"Who would do this?"

She shook her head. "I don't know. But the timing is troubling, isn't it?"

"I hurried off, unwilling to stand as her target for more barbs."

"Unless we regain the accounts we have lost, we shall soon find ourselves in serious peril," she exclaimed as I departed the counting room.

That night I withdrew into the counting room at the wharf, bent on finding some remedy and proving my mother's suspicions of Maryann unfounded. By the flickering light of a candle, I pored over the ledgers, compiling a list of potential clients who might salvage our dwindling prospects. But my thoughts returned, again and again, to that note. Who had sent it? Was it connected to the person who made the deliberate false rumors about my father or tied to the transaction of indigo that never got picked up, possibly?

The hours slipped by unnoticed as I worked, the sounds of the wharf fading into the hush of night. At some point, exhaustion overtook me, and my head settled onto the open ledger. In my restless sleep, a terrifying vision unfolded. My mother had packed all our belongings into crates, her movements deliberate and resigned. Then suddenly, I was at the warehouse where we stored goods. It was empty, its floors bare. The docks were eerily silent without a single vessel moored at the wharf. Then suddenly, I stood aboard *Providence*. The vessel was in disrepair, its sails tattered, the deck groaning beneath my feet. Walking upon the empty deck of the ship, my father emerged from a thick mist, his face etched with disappointment.

"You failed to meet your duty," he said, his voice cold. "You let everything fall apart because you were selfish." His accusation echoed, reverberating through the docks.

I opened my mouth to protest, to explain, but no words came. Then I saw Maryann near the docks, walking away. As I stood alone on the ship, it disintegrated beneath me, and I fell into a cold abyss.

I jolted awake, my chest pounding and my forehead damp with sweat.

The candle on the desk had burned to a nub, its last flickers barely clinging to life. The duress I'd been under was beginning to take its toll and it reminded me of why I hated such obligation.

How it snuffed out your individuality and left you beholden to others. My father had been gone far too long. If he could've come back, he would've made all my troubles go away. As I sat staring at the wall, I clung to one fragile thought: there had to be a way forward. We had to reclaim what was slipping from our grasp before it was too late. Otherwise, any future with Maryann would vanish, and I'd be left with nothing left but failure.

Chapter 20 (October) – Lost Accounts

That week, driven by resolve, I set out to win back the accounts we'd lost. I made my way to Faneuil Hall Market, where rows of wooden stands brimmed with root vegetables and late autumn fruit. I got wind of the sharp bite of vinegar, tobacco, and fish mingled with the sweetness of dried spice. The market bustled with the voices of eager sellers, the clatter of moving carts, and the footsteps of all manner of folk. A man weaving through the crowd approached and passed me a pamphlet. I read the small print which detailed an upcoming play at Federal Hill Theater: *She Stoops to Conquer.* I tucked the advertisement in my pocket, recalling that Maryann had been wanting to go to the theater.

I deftly made my way through the chaotic crowd and approached a booth where Mr. Franklin, a longstanding customer of the family business of over a decade, was busy selling his goods. He was well established and owned a small warehouse near the wharf where he stored his sugar, spices, and fruit we imported for him from the West Indies. Though he was always welcoming, he was also a cunning businessman. He could be intimidating and a tough negotiator, though his support had been unwavering, until now. When I approached, he paused only briefly before returning to assist a customer. I waited impatiently as the transaction dragged on. I stood close, pretending to be interested in what he was selling, though my mind was anxiously wanting to convince him to remain with our company. Once he was through with his customer, he looked at me with his lips curved slightly upward and a raised brow. I approached.

"Caleb," he started, "I know why you're here. I'm sorry, but this isn't personal."

"I understand, Mr. Franklin. But you've been doing business with my father for ten years. We've always been reliable. When have we ever under-delivered?"

He hesitated, the meaning of my words clearly giving him pause. "You haven't," he admitted. "But things are more competitive now, and I need more room for profit."

"What price are they offering you on your goods?"

"They've offered a rate twenty percent lower than yours," he said reluctantly.

Twenty percent lower than our rates was a significantly lower price. I had to act quickly if I wanted to keep his business. I leaned in slightly, my tone firm. "What if I told you I could give you a ten percent discount on your shipments? We've never failed you, and we won't raise prices unless our costs rise. That is something the Standard Shipping Co. hasn't promised, I am sure."

Mr. Franklin tilted his head, weighing the offer. For a moment, hope rose within me. He studied me, then said faintly. "Son, I have already signed the contract. I can't go back on my word. I am sorry."

"I suppose everyone is true to themselves these days!"

There was obviously no reasoning with him any longer, so I abruptly left the booth, heading to meet with other accounts. As I came to Dock Square, a crowd had gathered near a post, the chatter tense with anticipation. As I moved forward, the source of their fixation came into view—a man being carried away by a constable.

"This man has been charged with unlawful entry and thievery," the constable announced.

I recognized the man from somewhere, but I couldn't quite recall as the constable stood behind him gripping his arm hard and dragging him towards the nearby gaol. The man attempted to get free, but the constable held him firm while the crowd gathered to take a long look at the accused. A sick feeling curled in my stomach. The fate of the man surely seemed bleak, facing imprisonment, and though it was less common nowadays, possibly a public whipping. He was a testament of how low life could get if you took the wrong turn. As I made my way to meet with other accounts, the image of the man lingered: his struggle, his shame, and the thought of him being placed in a dark, dingy cell for an extended time.

Discouraged by the initial letdown from Mr. Franklin and shock of the public arrest, I spent the rest of the day visiting other accounts, only to be turned down one by one, from the rum distiller, Mr. Mackay, who bought molasses, to Mr. Lowell, who relied on us for textiles. The Standard Shipping Company's prices were too low for us to compete with, contracts already executed. Rejection upon rejection had stacked like bricks in an ever-growing wall of bitterness. I felt for the advertisement in my pocket and contemplated the questions that gnawed at the back of my mind: Was my mother right about my pursuit of Maryann? How much longer could the company endure losses? Unfortunately, the answer seemed clear. With one ship already sold and the loss of numerous accounts, the Atlantic Shipping Co. was no longer on steady ground.

Chapter 21 (November) – Invitation to the Theater

With the sun scarcely up, I paced in the parlor room, dwelling on the previous week's defeats. I hadn't informed my mother, since those accounts were already lost in her mind. Telling her I was turned down would only solidify her anxieties and encourage her to blame me for my pursuit of Maryann. Afterall, this was not Maryann's doing. Her father was a successful and prominent businessman. There were others pursuing the West Indies as well. As for my pursuit of Maryann, it was heading in the right direction and truly the only thing that was at the moment. At last, I sat at the desk, where the invitation I had written for Maryann to join me at the theater lay waiting. As I concluded the invitation, Charlotte entered the room, her inquisitive nature unrelenting as she peeked over my shoulder.

"Are you writing to Maryann?" she asked, her all-knowing look frustrating me.

"Nothing gets past you, does it?"

"Well, I just thought…"

As I heard those words, my blood began to simmer. "Just say it."

"That you would end your pursuit of her."

"Why would I do that?" I asked, shaking my head.

"Considering the lost accounts, of course. That's not all. She was in the company of Charles at the Common. Sorry, I could not help but presume."

"She is at liberty to see him, as I am to see her. And as for the business obstacles, she's no part of it!"

She nodded her head slowly. Then she asked calmly, "May I suggest something?"

I said not a word.

"Knowing you, you'll probably just hand it to her directly. Are you aware that could be seen as improper? Even rude?"

I frowned, her words striking me as though I did not know how to handle the matter. "Improper? It's just an invitation. Besides, I'd hand it to their family servant, of course."

In truth, I hadn't thought much about how I'd deliver it until now, for I wasn't keen on the protocol.

She gave me a pointed look. "If I were you, I'd make it a bit more subtle than showing up at her house."

"Perhaps you're right," I conceded.

Charlotte left and began preparing breakfast as her usual routine. She was faithful to her duties. For once, it seemed she wanted to help rather than put me down. Her mention of seeing Maryann and Charles together continued to play in my mind. I quickly finalized the invitation and headed towards the Hayes residence. Apprehension visited me as I imagined Maryann's reaction. Would she be caught off guard or hopefully excited?

As I approached her house, I stopped as I noticed someone standing with a bouquet of white roses through the window of her home. As I focused, I recognized that it was Mr. Payne. Then someone else entered the room: Mr. Hayes. He approached Mr. Payne, placing his hand on his shoulder. Before I was seen, I turned and quickly walked away. I lumbered to a stone wall, where I sat down, gripping the invitation. Perhaps my sister was right. Perhaps I should have found another way to deliver the invitation. But doubts swirled in my mind. Not only did I have to compete with Charles Derby, but now Mr. Payne? Why was I pursuing her anyway? I contemplated. Surely, she was beautiful, authentic, educated, and disciplined, to say the least. But in the end, was I wasting my time? I was so perplexed. When we were together, we got along so well. There was something unexplainable, an unseen force that made being with her feel right. Yet I couldn't help but wonder if her affections were genuine. On the other hand, the only way to know if she felt the same was to continue to spend more time with her.

Needing a good middle person, I made my way to the sail loft at Long Wharf, where I found Owen stitching two sailcloths together, edge to edge. I saw him through the window, meticulously stitching, the ever patient and focused person he was. I tapped on the window and called out to him. After a brief spat with the foreman, he joined me.

"Sorry to bother you, Owen."

"Don't worry about it."

"Looks like you are working hard."

"Always. But you know what? I actually enjoy it. You know the sails we craft; they take a lot of time and patience. But it's a wonderful sight when they are completed and placed onto a ship's mast. A well-made sail is always ready for the wind to take it."

"I suppose you are right."

"What's on your mind?"

"I need your help."

"Anything for a friend. I needed this break," he said with a sigh. "Been working like a dog since morning."

"I need your cousin to give this invitation to Maryann."

"What's the invitation for?"

"The theater."

Owen paused, his eyes looking toward the ground.

"What is it?"

"You don't know what you're doing, do you? If you invite her and her family disapproves, this could be it."

"What do you mean?"

"The theater isn't fully accepted by every family in town," he explained. "The Hayes family…well, they're the type who might frown upon it."

"Maryann expressed her interest in the theater to me," I replied, though the conviction in my voice faltered as I thought about her parent's strictness.

Owen shrugged. "It's just risky. Maybe take her for a stroll along the waterfront."

I sighed, holding up the invitation. "I need to do something different than the norm. Can you give it to your cousin so she can pass it along?"

Owen grinned. "Of course."

He tucked the invitation into his pocket. "I'll see you around. And do tell me if she accepts. I wish the best for you."

Owen entered the building, picking up where he left off, I was sure. As for myself, I departed with my thoughts scrambling. Would Maryann accept my invitation? Would her parents approve of her going to the theater? I wavered, as my invitation was now in the hands of fate. Maybe this was all a mistake. But maybe it was my chance to deepen what we shared.

Chapter 22 (November) – The Theatre

About a week later, I was surprised to find a letter slipped under the door. The parchment was folded with a wax seal and the ink still fresh bearing my name. My heart pounded as I broke the seal and unfolded the letter.

Dear Mr. Thompson,

It is with sincere gratitude that I acknowledge your most kind invitation to the theater. I shall have the honor and pleasure of attending. I look forward to your company and conversation. Meet me at my home and we will take the carriage from there.

With kind regards, Miss Maryann Hayes

Maryann's gracious words stirred something deep within me. She had every opportunity to refuse. Surely, by now, she was aware of my family's recent business struggles and those that conflicted with hers, yet she had chosen to accept.

On the day of the play, I promptly headed out for the Hayes residence, adorned with my father's navy-blue coat, a crisp white shirt beneath it. I wanted to look my best. After all, this was my chance to impress Maryann in a way I hadn't before. As much as I wanted to relish this moment, the shadow of uncertainty loomed with questions surrounding who else was pursuing her. Still, I had to make the most of the moment. When I arrived, Mr. Boyle was already standing near the carriage.

"Hello Mr. Thompson. Maryann will be out shortly."

"Thank you, Mr. Boyle."

Without much for conversation, I quietly waited near the carriage. Then after a few more moments, she exited her home. She was radiant and well-suited for the autumn chill, clad in a rich plum silk gown and a charcoal spencer jacket. Maryann looked at me, her smile bright like the sun glistening off the ocean.

"I hope you did not invite me just because no one else would go," she said.

"I had an entire list of candidates. But unfortunately, they all paled in comparison."

"Flattery, Mr. Thompson?"

"Let me be clear, I could think of no finer company."

We climbed in the carriage as the wheels began to roll along the cobblestone road.

"You remembered that I expressed interest in the theater. That's a trait any girl would admire."

"To be honest, I was surprised your parents allowed it."

She laughed lightly, a mischievous glint in her eyes. "They were quite against it, I promise you that."

"What changed their minds?"

She smirked. "Let's just say I can be persuasive when I need to be."

I could imagine the conversation, her quiet determination swaying even the firmest opposition. There was a way she balanced grace with quiet defiance, challenging social expectations while still embodying everything society expected of her.

As we made our way through the crowded streets, the carriage turned near the Old State House, where a gathering crowd had formed. We slowed down to pass by as the crowd spilled out into the street. A town crier stood atop a makeshift platform, ringing his bell with methodical vigor, drawing all within earshot to listen. Curious, I leaned forward through the window of the carriage. The crier's voice rang out over the hum of the crowd.

"Hear ye, hear ye! Rumors abound from the great war abroad…whispers about the Napoleonic struggle!"

Mr. Boyle flicked the reins to continue forward as an opening made way.

"Please halt the carriage!" I yelled.

The servant pulled the reins back, and we stopped abruptly.

"I need to hear this report. I will be right back."

Maryann's eyes were wide open as she nodded. I hurried out of the carriage and made my way to the edge of the crowd.

The town crier continued, "Though no official paper confirms it, there is word from across the Atlantic! A mighty sea battle has been fought off Cape Trafalgar, on the twenty-first of October! Sixty ships did clash upon the waves! Admiral Nelson and the British fleet have dealt a crushing blow to Bonaparte and his allies! Reports tell of over four thousand lost among the French and her allies, with British losses but a fraction in comparison!"

A hush settled over the crowd, all ears drawn to the gravity of his words.

"However, his Majesty's ship *Victory* suffered grave damage, and the esteemed Lord Nelson has perished in the fight. Notably, significant losses were also reported aboard *Colossus* and *Royal Sovereign*, among other vessels engaged in the action."

The world around me stilled as I realized *Royal Sovereign* was the ship my father was forced onto. The murmur of the crowd dissolved into a distant hum. My feet felt rooted in place, as though the news paused time. As the crier concluded his announcements and stepped down from his platform, I quickly approached him to find out more.

"Sir, wait!"

The crier seemed taken aback by my vigor, though his countenance bore the weary patience of someone who had seen such excitement before. "What is it, young man?"

"Do you have any more reports? Specific names?"

He shook his head. "Just the notable ones. Why do you ask?"

"My father was conscripted into the Royal Navy and taken aboard the HMS *Royal Sovereign*."

The crier's face grew somber. "Terrible news, truly. I'm sorry, lad. They say the *Royal Sovereign* led the charge and lost her main mast. Over a hundred lives, gone. But don't lose heart. These are not official reports."

Before I could respond, a voice from the dispersing crowd muttered, "Maybe he wanted to join the British. He was a Loyalist during the war, was he not?"

I turned sharply, anger flaring hot in my chest. "Wanted to join the British?" I snapped. "And abandon his family?"

The man held up his hands in a placating gesture. "I'm sorry, son. I only meant if he was once loyal, perhaps his position made things complicated. You don't know his fate yet."

I walked away before I did something foolish with my anger still burning. But beneath the anger lay something heavier—dread. I entered the carriage, and we carried on.

"Is something troubling you?"

"I don't know to be honest. I am sorry. I needed to hear that report about the Napoleonic War. My father was taken aboard a British man-o-war. And…"

"I understand, do you want to continue to the theatre?"

"Of course, let's go," I said, looking at Maryann.

When we arrived at the theater, a line had already formed, patrons gathering in clusters, some adjusting gloves and hats, others engaging in animated conversation. The venue itself was grand, its brick façade aglow with the flicker of whale-oil lamps. Inside, the stark division of class was unmistakable: gilded private boxes held the town's elite, while the working class jostled for space in the galleries above. Our seats were positioned in the pit, placing us somewhere between the two groups.

As we settled in, my gaze scanned the audience. The presence of Boston's wealthiest was unmistakable, their fine attire and air of superiority setting them apart. My thoughts wandered to my father's journal, to the enigmatic figure he had written about. To the threatening letter that my family should leave town. If that man was present at the theater, I wouldn't even be able to recognize him, I thought.

"Is this what you expected?" Maryann asked, watching me closely.

"Not quite," I admitted, still lost in thought.

I quickly refocused and turned the question back to her. "How about you?"

She smiled joyously, looking around as though she was taking notes. "It's more."

The play commenced with a lively comedy that quickly captivated the audience. Maryann was immediately pulled into the play laughing at every opportunity. But by the time the second act began I was all but fully disengaged. I found my focus slipping back to my father's state of circumstances with the words of the town crier looping in my mind. I dwelled on all the loose ends of the business, tasks and errands I had to do to keep pace with. It was all too much. Maryann's laughter diminished as she kept looking over to see if I was enjoying the play. She leaned toward me, her voice barely above a whisper.

"Would you rather go?"

"Of course not, I am here with you," I said, though I could hear the hollowness in my tone.

"You seem…distracted."

Despair coiled inside me. Here I was, sitting beside Maryann in a theater, a moment I should have treasured, yet I could not escape the gravity of my thoughts.

"Let's go," she said gently.

"Let's stay," I protested.

She got up out of her seat and held her hand out for mine. "Let's get some fresh air."

A few heads turned as we slipped out, murmurs of mild irritation drifting in our wake. I was speechless as I wondered if I had offended her or ruined her time. Outside, the cool late evening air carried the sounds of the town settling into the night.

"Let's take a walk," Maryann suggested.

I took a long look at her and grinned. I was impressed by her kindness.

We climbed back into the carriage, heading toward the Common. There, we strolled amongst the oaks and chestnut trees, our pace unhurried. For a suspended moment, I found myself absorbed in the quiet austerity of the season. The oak beside us stood bare against the night sky, its limbs reaching like famished silhouettes. Overhead, a half-moon hung pale, casting a gentle sheen across the worn paths and still branches. The Common was quiet, with only sparing evening wanderers moving through the dim evening stillness.

"I'm sorry," I said, breaking the silence.

"No need for an apology," she replied, her voice steady. "I understand."

"You are kind, Maryann."

"Your father is missing and endangered. And yet you still took me to the theater despite everything you're going through."

Her understanding set me at ease. "Thank you."

She nodded. "There can be other nights for the theater."

"Yes, surely, we can try again. When there are no interruptions," I replied, knowing well that a life without interruption was a fanciful and far-fetched notion.

Eventually, a question I had been trying to suppress forced itself to the surface.

"What do you think of Charles?"

She laughed softly. "Blunt, aren't you? Well…let me think."

I regretted asking the question the moment the words left my lips. I braced myself for a long list of his positive traits.

"He has a certain charm," she admitted. "He's competent with finances. My father likes him. My mother thinks he's the perfect suitor. But then again, she only sees what she wants to see."

"How long has he been courting you?"

She considered my question. "About eight months."

I nodded, processing her words. "What about Mr. Payne? I saw him at your house with flowers," I blurted. "When I came to give you the invitation myself, I saw him, so I turned back."

"Oh, you are too silly, Caleb. I often give him flowers from my garden. It's nothing. He is courting someone else, as you are aware."

"Oh, yes… I had forgotten he was courting someone else."

The evening ended as we both headed our separate ways. Mine to a home full of burdens and hers to a home full of stability. Though the events of the night did not play out as expected, they ended up as good as they could have, given the circumstances.

Maryann was gracious towards me, and her support made my father's plight more bearable.

That night, searching for solace about my father, I reached for his journal.

One entry, written five years earlier, caught my attention. He described a journey to the West Indies, one that had taken a perilous turn.

October 21st, 1800

A sudden storm swept in on us the previous night, the wind howling violently through the rigging, waves crashing over the bow. The men held their posts, their faces pale from the tossing yet resolute. The gale was hitting us hard, such as that it tested our will. Though it proved one of the fiercest storms we had ever met, we bore it by standing fast at our stations and keeping watch for one another, even at the risk of our own lives. After the rains steeled and the men made necessary repairs, I sat back in my quarters contemplating what we had endured. Though terrifying as it was, it taught me, with self-sacrifice, there was always a way through.

I closed the journal, the inked words still lingering in my mind, like a distant beacon on a darkened horizon. I was in a storm in my own life, and it seemed there was no end in sight. But perhaps, as my father had written, there was a way through, if only I could find it.

Chapter 23 (November) – Fire on The *Providence*

The following night, I met Owen at the Green Dragon Tavern, the low murmur of conversation punctuated by bursts of laughter filling the room. A fiddler played a lively jig, a flutist carrying a tune alongside.

"Just ale tonight, Caleb?"

"Yes, I need to be on my best behavior," I replied with a smirk.

"How did the theater go?" he asked, lifting his tankard.

"Well, we ended up going to the Common. Let me correct the record. We went to the theater first, then to the Common."

"What happened?"

"I wasn't in the right frame of mind. Before we made it to the theater, I overheard the town crier make announcements about the war between France and Britain. The ship my father was on took heavy damage and there were many casualties aboard."

"I grieve for you, Caleb. I cannot conceive of what you suffer. Are there further particulars?"

"Nothing about my father."

Owen remained quiet.

"Maryann was the one who prompted us to go. She could see that I was in another place."

Owen smirked. "If it's any comfort to you, I think you might be positioning yourself nicely. I mean, she accepted the invitation. Then she forfeited her fun for your sake."

"She was kind. I hope you are right."

We drank, reminiscing over memories of our younger years, trading tales of mischief and youthful aspirations. After a few more drinks, we departed, slipping out into the cold night. As I went my way and Owen his, I ventured through the lantern-lit streets, the familiar quiet of the hour settling in. I walked for a while before heading home right away when a sudden and loud voice shattered the calm as a man I thought I recognized came running towards me.

"Caleb! Your father's ship is on fire!" the man yelled.

His words hit like a cannon blast to my chest. Though what he said made me unsettled, I did not immediately take any action.

"Hurry, *Providence* is burning!"

He grabbed my arm, and we sprinted for the harbor, my shoes hammering the gritty road while the State House bell clanged in the distance. As I approached Long Wharf, the acrid scent of burning wood filled my lungs. Ahead, violent flames roared to life with terrifying speed, an orange and reddish glow flickering against the night sky. I dashed along the dock, weaving past onlookers who merely gawked at the blaze. Leaping aboard the ship, I found the deck pump by the main hatch, yanked out its wooden bung, and heaved at the lever, but only a trickle spilled forth. Sparks showered the deck, the air thick with smoke that burned my throat. A sailor rushed to my side, then another, with three of us straining the lever. Then the pump finally sent a steady jet across the planks. More hands arrived carrying leather buckets, forming a line to douse the spreading flames.

Sailors, longshoremen, and townspeople took turns at the pump, while I shifted to flinging seawater onto smoldering sails and rigging. We'd corralled the main blaze, but pockets of flame still licked along the deck. Only when the fire brigade arrived, dragging their tubs and a fresh line of leather buckets, did the last embers hiss out. Spent and blister-handed, I looked around at the men who were beside me: a mix of neighbors, rival crews, and strangers bound for the moment by shared relief.

"Thank you," I said, my voice hoarse. "You helped save my father's ship."

"If you hadn't inspired us, it may not have turned out as fortunate as it did."

Catching my breath, I noticed a tall, thin figure step onto the ship forward, his lantern casting large shadows across the scorched deck. It was the port watchman. His presence was as unwelcome as the fire itself. His skinny frame was swathed in an ill-fitting frock coat, his battered tricorn hat doing little to conceal his perpetual scowl.

"How in the world did this happen?" he demanded, suspicion lining his tone.

"I don't know," I answered, forcing my breath to steady. "One of these men informed me of the fire."

The watchman's gaze swept over the gathered men. "Did anyone see anything?"

Not one word came from anyone.

"Someone must have witnessed something," he pressed, his irritation growing.

Still, no one spoke.

The watchman continued to saunter around the deck, observing the aftermath. I followed close, wondering if I too might catch sight of something amiss. We continued around the captain's quarters. The door was open, and the fire was out, so he ventured in, avoiding his head from being singed from an ember. I followed. There before us was a collective mess of my father's charred desk, some burned rope, and in the center of the room, shards of broken glass from a lantern scattered atop remnants of cloth.

He muttered under his breath before crouching near the singed remains, picking up the rope, lifting it to his nose. He straightened, his expression grim.

"Residue from pitch," he said.

He then pushed his stick against what appeared to be a broken lantern atop pieces of burnt cloth. He pulled his stick up and sniffed.

"Whale oil," he said.

"What is this?"

"Looks like the rope was used to start the fire. It burned slowly, then when its twine broke, this lantern, which was likely lit and full of whale's oil, fell on this cloth. A slow burn. Enough time to get in and out before anyone noticed," he suggested.

"This must be from a competitor," I said.

"Possibly," he countered, his eyes narrowing. "You are quite fortunate this ship is not completely sunk."

"I'm lucky I arrived quickly enough."

"Where were you when you heard of this?"

"I was walking near Dock Square."

"Where were you coming from?"

"The Green Dragon."

"What time did you leave?"

"Umm…I'm not certain," I admitted. "The fire must have started shortly before I left."

"Was anyone else with you when you left?"

"Yes. My friend Owen. Well, we went our separate ways after we exited."

"No one was with you… Hmm, convenient, isn't it?"

"What are you trying to say?"

"Just performing my duty," the watchman said, lifting his chin. He lingered for a bit, then asked, "Who informed you of the fire?"

"That man over there," I said, pointing toward a sailor on the ship.

"This is true," the sailor replied.

The watchman studied me for a moment, his expression making my soul ache. "Would your friend be able to confirm the time you left?"

"Of course. But I must say, this is absolutely absurd!" I retorted. Yet at that moment, I began to become nervous as I wondered what Owen could recall.

The watchman didn't respond. Instead, he addressed the crowd. "If anyone learns anything, report it to me or the constable immediately."

With one final glance in my direction, the watchman turned from the wharf and made his way toward King's Street, no doubt bound for the Green Dragon on his crooked errand. As he disappeared, the tension among the men eased, and they began to scatter. I let out a long breath, brushing soot from my sleeves. At that moment, it struck me how close I had come to losing my father's ship and with it, the very life of our business.

As I lingered on the docks, my eye caught a dim light burning in an upper window of the India Wharf building across the way. There, a whale-oil lamp flickered, casting long, wavering shadows that revealed a solitary figure watching. I marked it carefully: second floor, fourth window from the right. While the men drifted off into the night, I remained uneasy, wondering if others had seen something they dared not speak of.

Chapter 24 (November) – Setbacks and Accusations

First thing the following morning, I made my way to the Boston Marine Insurance office, located near the wharf. My father, stern as he was, had been a man of foresight and meticulous in his affairs. Fires were an inevitability in the harbor—too many ships, too much timber, too many chances for an accident. Knowing this, he had taken precautions, securing insurance for his vessels should a catastrophe strike while it was docked. Now, in the wake of the fire, that foresight was the only thing standing between us and ruin.

Heavy gray clouds added to my already morose mood, my thoughts tangled with what lay ahead. Without that ship, our business was left crippled. And without the claim, there would be no funds to rebuild, no way to salvage what was lost.

The office was a tall, three-story, narrow, but dignified, federal-style building. Whale-oil lamps flanked the doorway as I pushed open the heavy wooden door. The quiet scratch of clerks' quills filled the room as they bent over, calculating and recording diligently. Framed maritime prints and a chart of shipping routes hung on the walls, a good reminder of where the stream of revenues derived. As I approached a counter, a few heads lifted, their expressions mixed between sympathy and suspicion.

"Caleb," one of them said, his voice measured. "We heard about your father's ship."

"Word travels fast, I suppose," I replied, keeping my tone even. "I'm here to file a claim."

The clerk nodded slowly. "One moment," he replied, then disappeared into the back.

Hoping the transaction would go smoothly, I waited amidst the rustling of ledgers and the faint sound of quill pens tapping against wooden desks. Moments later, a man of refined appearance approached, his silk waistcoat impeccable, his starched collar standing at attention like a sentry. He was the owner, Mr. Winthrop, who had made a fortune on the perils of the sea but had likely never set foot on a ship himself.

"The Atlantic Shipping Company, am I correct?" he asked, his tone professional.

"Yes, that is correct" I said, straightening slightly.

"This morning, we received word of the fire. I have already reviewed your father's policies. He was thorough in his coverage. Fire, ship rot, vandalism, and weather-related damage are all covered under the contract."

I nodded. "How do we get the claim initiated?"

The owner folded his hands, his expression serious. "Well, hold on. We are aware of certain circumstances surrounding the fire that give us hesitancy. Due to this, we cannot honor a claim at this time. The matter will require further investigation."

A chill ran through me. The watchmen had already been insinuating I was involved somehow and now this. "What circumstances? Someone lit our ship on fire!"

His gaze was steady, unblinking. "There is reason to believe that this fire may not have been entirely accidental. As you are aware, deliberately setting fire to a ship for financial gain constitutes fraud."

The atmosphere shifted around me, tightening. "That's absurd. Why would we do that? In fact, I was nowhere near the ship when the fire started. I had just left the tavern and was on a walk when I was informed. There are people who can vouch for my whereabouts."

The owner sighed, as though my protest was an inconvenience. "We have the right to conduct our own investigation before we pay out."

I stiffened, anger stirring within me like a gathering storm. "I find this beyond belief!"

He held up a hand, his tone smooth. "Young man, I would caution against dramatics. It is well within reason. Your father's absence has left your business vulnerable. Others claim your business has been struggling to compete. A desperate family might see insurance as their way out."

I clenched my fists and stared at him.

He waved a hand dismissively. "Until the investigation is finished, your claim is denied."

I took a step closer. "You've already made up your mind, haven't you?"

He met my eyes. "We will notify you in writing once we reach a disposition," he said calmly. "And of course, you have the right to appeal. But can I mention one suggestion? I would back off and let the process play out, given all the circumstances."

I had no choice but to leave, though my body ached to fight against the injustice. The continuous misfortune was crushing: the fire, the rumors, the slow unraveling of my family's reputation and livelihood. I hurried through the streets, away from the wharf and past the familiar market. Yet nothing seemed real. It was as if I was wading through a thick fog, my fate playing out before me with every step. And worst of all, I knew that once word of this reached Maryann, she would have every reason to turn away from me. If no one would clear my name, I'd have to do it myself. And I knew exactly where to start.

I soon came upon The Bell in Hand Tavern looking to find the mix of sailors, carpenters, and longshoremen who helped to put out the fire. I made my way through the dimly lit room, around long communal tables scarred by years of abuse and low timbered ceilings obscuring my vision. Though it was still early in the day, I spotted an unruly group amidst the passersby and recognized a few faces of the very men I sought. They stood, tankards in hand, their laughter carrying above the clamor as I approached.

"Can I buy you all a round?" I asked.

"Aren't you the young man from the other night?" a sailor asked, his body swaying slowly.

"Yes, good memory!"

"We'll have some rum," a longshoreman said, with a chorus of agreement that followed.

I ordered a round for the group. My opportunity was ripe, as they were certainly already loose to talk.

"You made a quick, wise decision going for the deck pump that night," a sailor said.

"I was lucky to have your help," I replied, raising my tankard.

"Well, we didn't want our ships going up in flames next!" another jeered, prompting laughter.

When they settled down, I sat down to appear as though I was to stay for a while.

"No one saw anything unusual at the docks before the fire?" I casually inquired.

"We were all in here," one man admitted. "Except for Silas. He's the one who told us."

Silas sat at the edge of the group, his gaze lowered when he was mentioned. I ordered another round, determined to loosen his tongue. After another few rounds, switching subjects and chattering with the men, I managed to catch Silas alone and half seas over.

"If not for you, things could have been much worse," I said.

He nodded. "It could have been ugly."

"Bellamy's men," I said, lowering my voice. "They weren't at the docks last night."

He took a long drink, then said, "Well, not unusual, I suppose." He sipped another drink of rum.

"Did you see any of them around that night?"

He sighed. "Caleb, sometimes I see things I'd rather not. The fire…that's dangerous to us all. But I tend to mind my own business…about what men do."

"So you did see something," I pressed.

He leaned closer. "If you say you hear it from me, I will deny anything you say and make you look foolish."

"Of course, I won't say a word."

"There were some men near Mr. Bellamy's ship before the fire went ablaze. Nothing I'd call ordinary. But I'm not saying they did it."

I nodded, thanking him quietly. I had a few more drinks with the men then departed before I too found myself slurring my words. I had gained just the piece of information I needed. But that meant I had to look into Mr. Bellamy's operations a little further…and that I feared could cost me more than I was ready to pay.

Chapter 25 (November) –
Dead Ends and Broken Bones

The following night, while everyone was deep asleep, I put on my father's coat and prepared myself for anything that would come my way. I was determined to keep watch over the Bellamy & Co. ships and, if possible, find out if they had anything to do with the fire. But before I made it out of the room, Jameson leaped up from bed.

"I want to go with you, brother."

"I don't need your help."

"If you leave without me, I will wake everyone up."

Like myself, he had a persuasive and risky side about him. And that's what worried me.

"Fine, but listen to everything I say. We are just going to scope things out at the wharf."

He nodded enthusiastically then got quickly dressed.

It was a cold night. The docks of Long Wharf were dimly lit, a few whale-oil lanterns set sparsely along the length of the pier. Ships were docked, their masts swaying like restless phantoms. The windows of the warehouses were pitch black, the merchants and workers gone home for the night. We climbed aboard *Providence*, the charred mast of my father's ship, a reminder of the dangers we were now facing. We remained observing, waiting for any activity that would expose a culprit. The docks continued to grow quieter as the night wore on, the usual activity dwindling to a few meandering figures near the entrance to the wharf. Hours passed in silence as the ship rocked, its rigging creaking softly with the moving tide, the cold air chilling us to our bones. We lay on the deck waiting, the stars overhead gleaming like scattered diamonds.

"Do you see that star right there?" I said, pointing to a bright star visible in the northern sky.

"Yes."

"That is the North Star. Seafaring men call it *Polaris*. It never leaves its station. A ship may set its course by it, as certain as any chart."

"It definitely looks no different than the rest."

"Well, its purpose is, while all the others wheel about in their courses, it holds fast. That is why it is the sailor's truest friend. Find it and you'll always know the way north."

"Father taught you this?"

"He did."

"Why do you resent him so much?"

I looked over at Jameson. He was fond of me and that bore responsibility. I thought about what to say, so as not to burden him with my own.

"I suppose because I am the oldest, he put heavy expectations on me. And that came with some rigor. But let's not dwell."

We continued to hold quiet conversation, when well past midnight, something finally piqued our interest.

We heard a carriage approaching near a Bellamy & Co. dock. But from our vantage point, we couldn't make anything out, so we positioned ourselves toward the bow. We crept, the remaining crates and darkness of the night shielding us from being seen. As we observed, we noticed men were loading cargo onto the carriage. Their bodies were scarcely exposed by a glowing lantern. Then it struck me.

I turned to Jameson, whispering, "They're smuggling."

"What do we do?"

"This explains why the customs officer was on the ship a few months back," I murmured. "Let's go."

Jameson nodded. We meant to leave quietly. But before we could slip away, one of the sailors spotted us, pointing towards our ship. We heard some muffled chatter; then suddenly, a group of men headed our way. We scrambled and hid amidst the crates that were scattered and disheveled from the night before. The men reached the docks near our ship, then continued toward the gangway where the docks met the ship. We remained quiet, hoping they would leave, but then they walked up the gangway and boarded the ship. With each step, the hollow thud of their boots upon the planks set my nerves on edge.

"I saw them near the bow," one of the men said.

My stomach sank. Knowing what was coming, I had to get Jameson off the ship. We stood still as two men passed us.

"Go," I said, giving Jameson a slight push.

He sprang to his feet and bolted, leaving the men momentarily frozen in place. Then, I dashed toward the gangway, my steps drumming an insistent beat on the wooden planks. Jameson was already off the ship and running away from the harbor. Behind me, John and his companion scrambled for traction, their movements slow against the slick boards.

As I rushed toward the head of the wharf to catch up to Jameson, I found myself face to face with two men whose grim expressions promised violence. Before I could react, one of them lunged forward and grabbed my arm, his grip as cold and unyielding as the night itself. I struggled to get loose, but then another one of the men grabbed my other arm as they forced me away from into the shadows.

"What were you two doing?" one of the men growled.

"Let me go!"

"Tell us or we will beat it out of you."

I swallowed hard. "We were watching you."

They exchanged glances, smirking. "A rare honest answer."

"But unfortunately, that won't save you," the other man sneered before driving his fist into my stomach.

The impact left me without breath as I lay on the ground writhing in severe pain. Before I could recover, a boot crashed into my ribs. I instantly felt a deep regret for snooping, my foolishness compounding the stinging pain in my body. I was powerless, inadequate, and could only imagine the worst was still to come.

"Please leave me alone!" I shouted, whincing from the pain.

Then a voice shouted from beyond us as another man approached. "Knock it off!"

I recognized John Lowe stepping towards me, his menacing stature towering over me. The men backed off as he stood there, watching me squirm.

"He admitted to spying on us."

John, clutching the fid on his belt, loosened it and brought it close to my neck. "Caleb," he said in a sinister voice, "why are you poking your nose where it doesn't belong?"

I cleared my throat, trying to steady my voice. "We thought you had something to do with the fire."

John let out a dry, humorless laugh and stood up. "Well, it wasn't us."

One of the men came towards me, clearly ready to continue my punishment. But John placed a hand on the man's shoulder.

"Let him go."

The man hesitated, then nodded. I slowly struggled to my feet, clutching my side. John stared at me, his eyes blending in with the dark night.

"If you breathe a word of what you saw or the little beating you got, we'll find you," he warned.

Then they left.

I slowly staggered back to my feet and to where Jameson veered off, but he was gone. I continued to saunter, grasping at my side, when I heard someone wailing down the street. I feared it was Jameson as I got closer to where the yelling came from. I slowly continued my search, arriving at the building where I thought the awful screaming was coming from. A sign outside read *Dr. Brown, Consulting Physician & Apothecary*. I knocked hard, but no one came. I knocked harder; then surprisingly, the port watchman opened the door. I wondered why he was not near the wharf just a few moments ago. But realized it was because of what was happening in the other room.

The watchman waved me in, and I hurried towards the back where he was. There was a man, who I assumed was Dr. Brown, standing near Jameson, using sheers to cut his trousers. The wooden table, worn from years of use, now served as an operating surface as Jameson lay across it, sweat beading his forehead.

The man calmly continued, feeling along Jameson's leg, then wiped his hands on a stained cloth. An older woman entered the room holding a bottle of laudanum, poured it into a tin cup, and mixed a concoction. She brought the cup to Jameson's mouth.

"Drink. This will help with the pain."

Jameson drank, his eyes filled with tears.

"Give it ten minutes," Dr. Brown said.

Jameson panted and continued to breathe heavily.

"Hang in there, brother," I said, the guilt of his pain beginning to weigh on my conscience.

I held his hand in mine. I could tell the medicine was beginning to work as his breathing slowed. Then the doctor and the woman pinned Jameson down.

"Hold him steady," the doctor commanded.

The watchman and woman held him steady. With precision, the doctor wrenched his leg bone back in place as Jameson's raw scream rumbled through the house. After his leg was set, the woman wiped Jameson's forehead.

"It'll take weeks to mend," she muttered, placing a wooden splint and wrapping his leg in strips of cloth. "If it doesn't heal right, we'll have to take it off to prevent infection from taking his life."

I remained by Jameson, his breathing slowly getting calmer, his pain-drenched eyes fluttering shut as he fell asleep. About an hour later, a large coach-carriage arrived. We carefully lifted and laid him across a padded bench in the carriage. As we rode back to our home, each bump was a painful sting and reminder of what my mother's reaction would be.

When we reached the house, the watchman exited the carriage to knock on the door. A few moments later, my mother appeared, her expression shifting from shock to anger after the watchman explained what had happened. She then hurried out of the house to attend to Jameson. My sisters stood at the front of the house, wondering what the commotion was all about, while I stood by Jameson.

"What happened? Why were you out so late?"

"He broke his leg. The doctor set it. We need to monitor for infection."

"Tell me now, how did this happen?"

"They were chased," the watchman interjected.

She turned to the watchman. "Chased? By whom?"

The watchman sighed before turning to me, his expression stoic. "Would you like to explain what you were doing?"

"Tell us what happened!" my mother snapped, looking at me.

I stayed silent, though deep inside, I seethed with indignation. If the watchman was competent, he wouldn't have insinuated I had set my own father's ship on fire and actually done his job with competence. Even if I wanted to, I couldn't say anything; the haunting warning from John Lowe silenced me.

"Your lack of response leads me to have more suspicions about you, Caleb," the watchman said.

We lifted Jameson and laid him in his bed, his face still tense from the pain. Then the watchman left, without saying another word, assuredly his case against me building.

"I cannot find the words. I am more than disappointed in you," my mother said while I gave Jameson a long drink of whiskey.

"I'm sorry…"

"What were you up to?"

"I thought I could get to the bottom of who started the fire."

"Why did you take Jameson with you?"

"He insisted on going. I tried to stop him. I'm sorry."

"If your father was here, he would be ashamed."

"As if he was ever proud of me."

"Listen now! While you pursue your misadventures, you turn from your family's needs. You caused your brother to suffer for it. Caleb, that was most unthoughtful of you."

"Please. I will take care of Jameson tonight."

"I don't even know if I can trust you with that. I will be back to check," she replied as she stormed away.

Her words dug into me, reaching deep within my spirit. I had put my brother in danger, and for what? I wanted to leave, to escape, but I couldn't. I had to make sure he would recover. I stayed by his bedside until the whiskey and opium took hold again, and he drifted into sleep. As I sat beside him, I turned the events over in my mind, knowing one thing for certain. Someone wanted to destroy us and it was not Mr. Bellamy or John Lowe.

Chapter 26 (December) – The Most Dreaded News

The days that followed were filled with worry for Jameson's recovery. The days blurred together as I balanced the care of him and the bleak task of scouring the family accounts for any semblance of hope. I often found myself in my father's personal journal, when the day had retired and night fell, when Jameson had been fully asleep. Late into one night, I came across an entry from a day I had buried deep within my memories. In his unembellished hand, my father had written:

April 18th, 1790

Today Caleb began marking cargo for the first time. He finished one, then wanted to finish the rest until all the containers were completed. When he was done, I rewarded him with a shilling. But the most amazing thing was that he enjoyed the simplicity of making a mark on something.

I read the line twice, then a third time. My mind retraced all the moments I had resented his absence, all the quiet anger I had suppressed when his return felt more like a visit filled with demands and expectations than a homecoming. I began to recall that moment clearly. My father's smile and the warmth of the sun upon me. I remembered my eagerness to get all the markings on the cargo, wanting to make him smile again and again. I pictured myself on the deck and him handing me the coin, its reward a small payment compared to our connection, and for the first time, I understood. He was not a bad father. And I missed him.

When free moments during the day presented themselves, I found myself at the harbor, watching the ships drift in and out, their sails taut against the wind. My father's ship, once the pride of our business, was now decommissioned, hollow, a ghost of its former self. I waited, hoping that some good news might arrive with the tide.

Then, one evening, news of my father finally arrived. I had just returned home when a sharp knock echoed through the house. Upon opening the door, the port watchman stood before me, his somber expression leaving me hollow inside. Beside him was another man who was unmistakably a sailor with weathered and sun-darkened skin.

"Is Abigail home?" the watchman asked, clearly preferring to speak with her over me.

The solemn look on the watchman's face was more profound than usual. He clearly wasn't stopping by to hurl more accusations at me.

"Yes, one moment."

I fetched my mother and she hurried to the door, her face filled with anxious anticipation. "What is it?"

The watchman gestured toward the sailor. "This is Sam Pritchard. He served on the HMS *Royal Sovereign*. The same ship your husband was conscripted to."

She inhaled sharply, breathing slowly out. She stepped aside to let them in. I followed them into the parlor. The gravity of the moment was palpable. We had been waiting for months to hear anything about my father, and here was a man who had contact with him while he was away. Mr. Pritchard settled into a chair across from my mother. My sisters gathered in silence, the mood in the room thick with unspoken trepidation.

"I served aboard the HMS *Royal Sovereign* with your husband, as the watchman has stated," he began.

Mother's hands trembled slightly. "And how is he? Do you know?" she interjected, placing a worried hand on her face.

Sam's face softened with pity and sorrow. "That's why I'm here, ma'am. He was fatally wounded in the Battle of Trafalgar. He wanted me to give this to you." He reached into his pocket and pulled out a lock of hair, handing it to her.

Mr. Pritchard's words hung in the air, suffocating the oxygen. She held the hair in her hand, surely recalling when she had given it to him before he left. She sat motionless, her breath caught somewhere between disbelief and devastation. My sisters began to weep. I stood in stunned silence, as if my body was numb.

"I am so sorry to have to tell you this," Mr. Pritchard added, his voice heavy with regret.

My mother tried to speak, but the words failed her. She began to weep. She gathered herself and spoke quietly. "Where is his body?"

"We buried him at sea."

She stood abruptly, her eyes filling with tears. "Excuse me, I need to be alone." Without another word, she hurried into her room, the door closing softly behind her. My sisters walked back up the stairs slowly, still weeping to inform Jameson of the tragic news.

"If you need anything, please come by the constable's office," the watchman said, though his voice barely registered.

As the watchman and Mr. Pritchard began to leave, I followed, wiping tears from my face. "Mr. Pritchard, could I speak with you privately?"

He glanced at the watchman, who clearly disapproved by the look of his stern stare. "Of course, son," Mr. Pritchard replied.

The watchman pulled him aside. "When you are done, report back to me please. I would like to follow up on a few more details."

We returned to the parlor. The room had darkened with encroaching clouds outside, the flickering candlelight casting long shadows. Mr. Pritchard sat across from me, rubbing his hands together as if working up the strength to relive the past.

"I know this is a shock," he said gently. "I am sincerely sorry. Caleb, right?"

I nodded, my chest tightening.

"Your father became well respected on the ship. He was a true leader. Despite never wanting to be there, he became well-liked amongst the men. Many of the men did not want to be there. Including myself, that's why I had to leave."

"Did you desert?"

"Yes. I too was conscripted from the coastline in Nova Scotia. They could see I was a seafaring man. So they nabbed me. Just like many others on the ship. But the pay and the conditions were not worth that dangerous life."

"I can't imagine."

My father was well-respected amongst the men he worked with and also the community he lived in. But being respected by men he did not know made me feel a deep sense of guilt. *Was I the one who did not get along with my father?,* I thought.

"We became close over the months we spent together. He talked about you often. Though he seemed to have many regrets, often saying he had been too hard on you."

A sob clawed its way up my throat, but I forced it back. "I can't believe he's gone."

"It was clear he loved you."

I let the words settle, but with them came anger. Anger at those who put him in danger. I clenched my jaw. "Did he ever speak about how he was conscripted?"

"Aye, more than once. He never could fathom why they came for him in particular. Conscripting hands was common enough, especially those who were American. But he always reckoned they'd marked him out, as though some man had pointed the press gang his way."

A knot tightened in my stomach. "Did he mention anything strange before he left? About a new contract right before he departed from Boston?"

"Yes, yes, he spoke of it," he admitted. "Said it was a matter of regret, that he felt himself greedy for taking the offer. He feared it was all connected, yet he never knew for certain. It plagued his mind."

I leaned forward. "Did he describe the man who offered him the contract?"

He furrowed his brow. "I remember him saying the man was not familiar, that he had not laid eyes on him before. What struck him most was how finely he was dressed."

"Did he mention anything distinctive?"

He hesitated, then nodded. "Indeed, it was about the ring. Your father remarked how he could not keep from touching it with an anxious hand."

My pulse quickened. "Did he describe the ring by chance?"

"A red ring, he said, with some odd crest on it that looked like a bird to him."

My breath became harder to catch. *Red ring! Of course!* "But what about the bird? Did he say what kind it was?"

"Ah, yes, he did mention it. It escapes me now…oh, wait. He said it was some bird of prey, I think. But I forget exactly what he said. Forgive me, I cannot quite recall."

"Falcon!" I shouted, recalling the smudged word in my father's journal, *F—.*

Sam leaned back in his chair. "That's it!" He paused, crossing his arms, a wondering look on his face. "Son, what's the significance of all this?"

At first, I wanted to hold back what I learned. But Mr. Pritchard was clearly not a part of my father's conscription. Quite the opposite. He was a friend. "Since my father left, we've faced what would appear to be deliberate sabotage."

His face grew serious. "I was asked by the watchman to report after speaking with you. But be assured, I shall not divulge this matter."

"I would appreciate that. Thank you."

We sat in the parlor for another hour or so, speaking of their shared hardships, the camaraderie with the crew, the burdens they all carried being out at sea, forced away from their families. Eventually, as time waned and nothing else was left to be said, he stood, bidding me farewell. I escorted him outside. As his figure faded into the darkening night, I stood still, wondering if there was something else I could have asked. I rubbed my index finger, as though trying to find a sense of reality. I revisited the journal and the passage where my father's words were smudged. Yet, though I still had no clue who the man with the red ring was, I now knew what those words were.

Chapter 27 (December) – Old Granary Burying Ground

On the eve of my father's funeral, I spent the better part of the night contemplating all the things that could have gone another way. I recalled the last moment we spoke. Before he departed, we had an argument over my visits to the tavern. Regrettably, I recalled our last exchange of words, which were not so kind. Sorrow filled my heart as I relived that moment. I was in the counting room, away from the desk when he walked in.

"Unfocused as usual," he said calmly. But I knew anger was brewing within him.

"I just started to take a break. I've been staring at the ledger for a few hours now."

"Son, listen. You need to keep yourself out of the taverns and away from that cursed tipple."

"Well, I am here. Working as you wanted me to."

He walked over to me fumbling around in his coat, pulling out a compass.

"This is for you Caleb. Keep it as a reminder to always keep your path on track."

I looked at it with disdain and placed it into my pocket. Though it was a gift, it came with a subtle criticism.

He walked over to the ledger and sat down. As he studied the entries he began to rub his forehead, his patience thinning at each turn of the page.

"Caleb, what have you been doing with your time? These entries are incomplete," he said, shaking his head slightly. Then he quickly slammed the ledger closed and sprang out of his chair like a whale breaking the surface of the sea.

"I've had it with you! I can't count on you for anything. You don't focus enough for the ledgers. Your reputation is poor. So I can't rely on you to build accounts. And you don't want to do any hard labor so I can't ask you to help with the cargo, or do repairs on the ships. I really am disappointed in you."

"Well father, that's no surprise to me. You have never thought any good of me. I am happy to resign my position."

"Of course. I gave you an out and you took it quickly. I am afraid you are nothing but a wastrel!"

"If you weren't so harsh and lacking self-control, maybe I would try harder!"

"Get out! Now!"

I left the counting room. That day he departed out to sea. That was the last time I saw him.

But much has changed since then.

His captain's journal lay open before me, its pages filled by a hand both precise and disciplined. Page after page, he chronicled his voyages: the routes he charted through fog and gale, the terms he negotiated in foreign ports, the hard lessons taught by disease and death. There were stories of men lost overboard and men who drank themselves into ruin. But there was nothing—not a word—on how to navigate the waters that lay before me now. No entry titled: *What to Do When They Call Your Father a Traitor.*

What I did find, though, was a pattern. A record of a man who had shaped his life not by whim, but by persistence. A man who had left and returned, again and again, not in pursuit of glory, but for the sake of those waiting onshore. It was romantic only from a distance. Up close, it was toil and loneliness, and the constant company of risk.

The following morning, we gathered at the Old Granary Burying Ground under a sky layered thick with pewter clouds and bare trees with their empty branches swaying hypnotically. I passed the Smiths' graves, their tombs an ironic reminder of intertwined paths. Some of our relatives arrived, followed by Mr. Hall and his wife. A small number of people from town paid their respects, but many who knew him stayed home. The damage from the rumors, it seemed, had done its job. Any faith left in the family business had been destroyed with the news that my father had passed. However, Maryann arrived. Her presence felt like an act of quiet grace and was a reminder that despite the rumors, there were still those who could recognize decency when they saw it. My family gathered in front of the small group of mourners. Charlotte and Alice stood next to my mother on her left side, while Jameson, who was recovering without infection, held himself up by wooden crutches stood next to me on her right side. My mother stood straight, clasping her hands so tightly around a small bundle of her hair, rosemary and lavender bound with twine that her knuckles paled to ivory. She had quickly fallen into a deep depression once the news came, though now, she wore a stoic mask that had taken all her strength to assemble.

Since the sea had claimed my father's body, a headstone was all we had to mark his place among the deceased. As the minister spoke with a low voice and precise words, I tried to concentrate as I trembled from the pain. He spoke of courage, of duty and loyalty. For a moment, these virtues all appeared as punishments at the same time. The cost of courage being isolated. The cost of duty being one's freedom. The cost of loyalty, betrayal by those who you trusted.

When the minister stepped aside, my mother approached the grave. She spoke briefly, her voice flat but unwavering.

"Benjamin Thompson, was the most devoted man I know. I remember the day we met at the market. We knew each other but had not spoken to each other yet. He was kind and gentlemanly. I still recall the way he made me feel. When I was around him, I felt strong and respected. As we grew to know each other, I gained more respect for him with each passing day. Though he was out to sea often, and for long periods of time I knew where his heart was. Every fiber of his body, every choice he made, was for the betterment of his family. I stand before those few who still are willing to honor him, to say that he was a good man. If I have any parting words, it is to cherish the moments you do have with one another, as you may never know when is the last."

Then she laid the bundle at the foot of his gravestone, a final gesture to the man she had spent many years of her life waiting for while at sea.

When my chance came to speak, I stepped forward, suddenly aware of every eye upon me.

"My father," I began, "was a man of duty and honor."

I had intended to belabor these virtues, to leave the rest unspoken. But the unspoken truth about him pressed against my heart like a firm hand. I took a breath.

"There are those among us," I said, clearing my throat, "who have heard rumors about my father's loyalty during the war. I would like to put those rumors to rest."

The hush that followed was thick enough to touch.

"My father served not as a traitor, but as a spy. As one of Washington's own."

My mother's eyes turned sharply toward me. "Caleb," she said in a stern command, "what are you doing? Stop!"

But I could not stop. Not now. Not with the moment itself demanding the truth.

"I have proof," I said. "Among his belongings and records of his work."

A murmur rolled through the crowd, uncertain whether to rise into outrage or settle into disbelief.

"A spy? Has the young man gone mad?" someone scoffed.

"If he were a spy, we would have known by now," said another.

At that moment, my mother stepped in front of me and proclaimed, "The service has concluded. Thank you all for attending."

Then she turned to me and said, "I cannot believe you. He wanted all of that to remain in his past."

Then in a hurry, she escorted my sisters and Jameson from the gravesite, leaving me behind.

Mr. Hall stood there staring at me. It appeared as though he was holding back affirmations out of respect to my mother. I understood the look he gave me, empathetic and full of anguish.

As I walked away, rejected and disheartened, I heard someone say, "Perhaps it is true that he lit the fire himself."

I turned around to confront the person who said that, but the mourners had begun to disperse, even Mr. Hall and his wife.

As I had made my way to the harbor, Maryann caught up to me. Without uttering a single word, she walked beside me, her silent presence a subtle reminder that I was not as solitary as I had believed.

Then at the right time, after I had simmered down, she said, "If there is anything you need Caleb…"

"Thank you, Maryann. It's all too overwhelming. I need to spend a moment reflecting on this."

"I understand. Please take care of yourself."

I continued towards Long Wharf, the events of the day enough to anchor me down into the bottom of the ocean. The mist lay low on the water, blurring the line between sea and sky. I sat at the edge of the wharf and stared into the vast dark and deep blue sea, wondering why the truth about my father's past had to remain silenced.

"You deserved better than this," I said softly, the words dissipating as quickly as I spoke them. "They should know you as I now know you."

I sat at the dock's edge, alone with the ocean. Its depth and vastness, a reminder of the countless secrets that lurk beneath the surface, waiting to be brought to light. All my attention was now fastened upon the red ring, and how I might learn whose hand it belonged to.

Chapter 28 (December) – The Family Crest

The following evening, a heavy storm began to pour down torrential rain, turning the planks of Long Wharf into pools of water, while the ships in the harbor swayed gently like sleeping giants, half-vanished, in the heavy curtain of the downpour. I had little desire to return home as I stood staring out the counting room window. Even still, I had little motivation to study the family ledger any further. Deep down inside me, the nagging truth about my father's mysterious disappearance could never go away. Though I couldn't bring him back, there was still a chance to save his name. Especially since I recently learned more from Mr. Pritchard about the red ring.

I exited the storehouse building and walked the straight lane of State Street, dodging stevedores hauling crates away from the wharf. I continued until I reached the tight courtyard of North Square. Before me was the most prominent silversmith shop in Boston, located in the North End, established by Paul Revere himself and now transitioned to management under his son.

I stepped inside, cold and drenched from the downpour of the relentless rain. Inside were plates, trays, spoons, various types of molds, and other finished silver goods that were organized, hanging from walls and stacked atop shelves. A man standing near a bench raised his hammer in a steady rhythm and struck a glowing sheet, shaping it into the soft curves of a teapot's belly. What appeared to be an apprentice sat polishing a small metal box. Ahead at a counter was a man who kept a steady focus on me as I walked towards him.

"Hello, young man. How can I help you?" he asked, setting aside a ledger.

"Well, to put it plainly, I have an odd request. If I gave you a description of a family crest, could you tell me the name of that family? It's for a ring."

"That sure is an odd request. What is your name, son?"

"Caleb Thompson."

"A pleasure to make your acquaintance, Caleb. I am Paul Revere, Junior. I take it this must be of no small importance, seeing you've braved the heavy rain and chosen such words in your request. Before I speak further, may I ask plainly what the urgent matter at hand is?"

"I have to be honest. It's about my father. It's a long story. But the crest is in connection to someone who my father transacted with before he departed out to sea."

Mr. Revere took a deep breath. I was not certain he was considering kicking me out or reading me like a book.

"I know a sincere man when I meet him. Yours is a face worn by a long journey, and it shows in every line. Tell me about the ring."

"It's a family crest with a falcon snatching its prey. And it's red."

"Hmm… I'll have to dig through the ledgers and see if the mold still lies here or if this ring was even forged in this shop. Come back in a few days, and I'll tell you what I've found."

"Any information will be helpful," I said, giving him a long, steady look. I had respect for him. His father held a place of high regard, esteemed alike in our town and throughout the country. Yet he was humble and willing to help me out. I nodded, wished him a good day, and withdrew into the pouring rain. Though I wasn't sure if he would find anything, I had a small inkling of hope he would.

Chapter 29 (December) - Starting Over

After my visit to the Reveres' shop, I waited anxiously for what he might find. To avoid interaction with my mother, I often found myself at the harbor or stationed in my room. I could not understand her reluctance to let the public know about my father's occupation as a spy during the war. Maybe it was her way of honoring him or her attempt to put the pain she had endured away. Of course, grief could leave a person uneven. And in the days since my father's passing, my mother had become not so much uneven as unpredictable, with each passing hour seeming to usher in some new stage of exasperation or despair. This was, by any measure, understandable. But then there were other offhand but sharp remarks that clung to me. "You've been calling on Maryann quite often, haven't you?" she had asked one afternoon, her tone practically cheerful, though her eyes remained unblinking. At the time, I took the observation as little more than conversational debris. But now, with the time to think deeper about it, I began to see the remark in a different light—as if it were not casual at all, but deliberate and bitter.

It was in this state that a knock came at the front door. My mother greeted a visitor, a male figure by the sound of his voice. I heard footsteps towards the parlor where they carried on a discussion. Curious, I slowly crept down the stairs to listen further.

"How are you holding up?" asked the man whom I recognized as Mr. Hall.

"Unimaginable," my mother said in a serious and saddened tone.

"I can understand."

"Thank you for your support," she said. "There have been...more setbacks than I can count. And that is why I called you here. I would like to post an ad for the sale of the Atlantic Shipping Co. I need your help to draft the paperwork."

Mr. Hall went silent. He cleared his throat, then said cautiously, "Well, this is a monumental decision. While I appreciate your trust in my services, I am not sure if I could actually perform them without conflict."

"I understand you, Mr. Hall. The business still holds some value, even with *Providence* being in the shape she is in, she is repairable. We still have *Eleanor*, the storehouse, and the remaining accounts that have been established with contracts. With your help, we will have something to begin anew. Of the lawyers in this town, I place my trust in you most."

"Give it some days to settle in your mind. I'd have you sure of yourself before I help with the selling of the business."

"My mind is settled, Mr. Hall. With every day, the business falls further into disrepair. Have you heard the latest? Liam has given his resignation, if the news has not reached you yet. Please, help us."

"Very well. I shall see the contract made and the papers drawn. If the Thompson family has a need for me, then I will lend my hand."

"Thank you. We should place an ad in the paper while you draft the contract."

"I shall attend to this without delay. Until then, take good care, and should your family standin want of anything, I trust you will call upon me."

As soon as Mr. Hall left, I hurried down the stairs to the parlor room.

"Mother, we don't have to sell the business."

"I have contemplated this long and hard. This is our chance to start over. There is no more reason to hold on. It's time to move on," she said, her voice resolute.

"There must be some way to save it," I said. "We could find new partners and eventually repair the ship. We could…"

Her eyes turned slowly, with an angry gaze meeting me. If looks could topple empires, this one would have accomplished it.

"Why should you care so much about it?"

" *Why?*" I repeated, flustered by the question. "Because it's our business. Our family's future."

She let out a quiet, joyless laugh. "Let me be perfectly clear. For years, your father wore himself out in labor, while you squandered your hours with drink and gaming, appearing at the docks only when you hungered for money or absolution. And now, suddenly, you care?"

"You're not fair."

"No?" She pushed herself upright, though her hands trembled with the effort. "I think I know exactly what's driving this devotion. It's not the business you want to save, Caleb. It's your standing with the Hayes family."

I flinched; her words struck less like a slap.

"What do they have to do with this?"

"If the business folds," she said, "what future could you possibly offer Maryann?"

"I should leave you alone," I replied, then heading out of the room.

But as I reached the threshold, her voice followed me like a draft through a cracked window. "Why else would you care? You've never cared about anything that didn't serve yourself."

I left the house in outrage, aimlessly wandering the streets, watching thick clouds gather in the slate sky. I could feel my mother's words gnawing at the edges of my mind, demanding to be examined. Was she right? Was I only concerned for my own self-interest? Was my pursuit of Maryann all in vain? I had no answers. They lingered about me like unwelcome company, questions refusing to depart until I gave them an audience. One thing was certain; all my efforts to help the family business had failed miserably. All I could think was that, if Mr. Revere found nothing, I would face yet another dead end and with it, a deep despair.

Chapter 30 (December) – An Unpleasant Dinner

One afternoon, a knock at the door drew me from my daze, while I stood by the hearth in the kitchen after feeding the fire. Anticipating it was Mr. Hall with updates on the sale of the business, I hurried to open the front door only to find Mr. Boyle, the Hayes servant; cloaked, gloved, and framed perfectly by the winter sky, as if he were posing for a portrait rather than performing an errand.

"Miss Maryann requests the pleasure of your company," he said, extending a cream-colored envelope with the sort of formality typically reserved for weddings or declarations of war.

I took the envelope, opened it and read:

Dearest Caleb,

It would give me great pleasure to have you join us for dinner tomorrow at 3 o'clock at our home.

With the highest regard,

Miss Maryann Hayes

My spirit came alive as I read the invitation. The last time I saw Maryann was at the funeral, and every day since, I wondered how

I could see her again. A significant amount of time was also spent doubting if she would want to continue with me at all, now that my financial future was wrecked.

The servant offered a polite smile. "Shall I return with your reply, or would you like to consider the invitation further?"

"I accept and look forward to it."

"Well, then, we shall see you tomorrow," the servant replied.

I closed the door as he departed in a carriage.

I stood by the fire, holding onto the invitation. The turmoil and setbacks I had endured were heavy, yet there was still some veneer of hope left. I wondered where Maryann was at that very moment. I wanted to see her now, but I had to wait.

I left the house the following afternoon, anticipating an eventful day, eager to see Maryann. When I stood before the Hayes residence, it no longer intimidated me. Rather, it stood more like a monument to certainty than to pretense, with its bricks squared, its windows evenly spaced, its front door polished to a high shine. I knocked gently as my mind raced with nervous excitement.

The door swung open with prompt efficiency. "Welcome, Mr. Thompson," said Mr. Boyle, ushering me into the warm glow of the entry hall.

Maryann descended the stairs and stood at the far end of the hall, luminous in an ivory gown tailored to perfection. Her smile was the same one that had undone me many times before—warm and unassuming. Just by the look of her I was beginning to unravel.

"My heart is warmed by your company," she said.

"And mine by your welcome," I replied.

We made our way to the parlor and sat down in ornately designed, cushioned chairs. On top of a small tea table was the latest print of the *Boston Gazette*. I could not help but continue to observe as an advertisement was circled in ink that read: *To Be Sold. The entire Interest in the Atlantic Shipping Company, comprising a well-established...*

While everything from the furniture, the firelight, the spacing between us, was perfectly arranged, something felt out of order. That was when I began to panic. The Hayes family was expanding to the West Indies. Surely, her father was reading that ad, with interest to buy the business! Then, my heart dropped, and my mind flooded with doubt. Maryann had to know my family's business was for sale, and that was the reason she was inviting me over for dinner.

"How are you holding up?" Maryann asked softly.

I slowly gained my focus back. The advertisement was a sharp reminder of the position I was in, and truthfully, the position the Hayes family was in. "As well as can be expected," I replied, which was neither honest nor dishonest. It was simply the phrase one offers when the truth is unwelcome at polite gatherings.

"I admire your strength," she said. "It can't be easy."

"No," I said with a deep sigh. "It's not."

Before the conversation could travel further down a path that may have ended in confrontation, Mrs. Hayes entered the room, her crimson gown rustling like autumn leaves against the floor. Seeing her always required a moment's adjustment—a reminder that whatever hopes I had pinned to Maryann, they were to be measured against the lofty expectations of her mother.

"Mr. Thompson," Mrs. Hayes began, "we were sorry to hear of your father's passing. If there is anything our family can do, you have only to ask."

"Thank you," I replied, forcing a smile.

From beyond the hall came the sound of heavy footsteps descending the stairs. Mr. Hayes entered the room, his posture was as it always was: upright, unyielding, designed to suggest a familiarity with authority and consequence.

"Mr. Thompson, it must be a difficult time for your family."

"It is," I replied. "There are still many unanswered questions."

"As there always are," he said, nodding as if he, too, had been familiar with what I was suggesting by unanswered questions. "Our sympathies, of course."

"Thank you."

Mr. Boyle entered the parlor, breaking up the awkward and ironic formalities. "Dinner will be ready shortly," he said before retreating to the hall and down the back stairs that led to the basement kitchen.

Mr. and Mrs. Hayes departed while Maryann and I remained.

Maryann placed her hand lightly atop mine. "You'll get through this."

I offered a smile in return. Yet now, I was cautious to accept her kindness.

After a few moments, we were called to the dining room, where the table gleamed like a mirror, every utensil aligned with its twin across the way. Mr. and Mrs. Hayes took their seats, and as we waited, discomfort crept in like a draft beneath the door.

"Your father's ship," began Mr. Hayes, his tone light but his meaning sharp, "will it be repaired soon?"

From across the table, Maryann's foot began to tap on the floor, quick and uneven. I looked at her, then back to Mr. Hayes.

"Yes, I am confident it will be fully repaired after the insurance claim is processed," I said, keeping my answer as short and confident as possible.

"Of course, your father had insurance on the ship," Mr. Hayes replied, the curve of his mouth suggesting a bit of glee.

The first course arrived: turtle soup, thick and lukewarm. I swallowed each spoonful with the care of a man testing for poison. The conversation took a turn as Maryann changed the subject, from skating ponds during the winter to hunting parties. Unintentionally, she reminded me that an invitation to Charles to go hunting had been extended months ago, while mine had yet to arrive. The main course followed: venison with glazed carrots, mashed parsnips, biscuits, and cranberry sauce spiced with something unidentifiable.

"How is your mother?" Mrs. Hayes asked, her tone so gentle that I nearly mistook it for sincerity.

"She's holding up as best as she can."

"With all the disruption in *Providence*, have you encountered any difficulties fulfilling your contracts?" Mrs. Hayes inquired.

Maryann's fork clattered onto her plate. Without a word, she rose from the table and left the room. Shortly after, her mother followed, issuing whispered entreaties Maryann ignored. Mr. Hayes remained seated, his expression one of mild inconvenience, as if his daughter's outburst had interrupted his evening. Then Maryann's voice began to rise as the argument continued and I heard footsteps go up the stairs.

"I'll be right back," he said, disappearing from my presence.

The room was narrowing around me as I was left alone, leaving me to my deep unease. It was then that I began to further question Maryann's intentions. The timing of the invitation was right after the ad was published and not before. Mr. Hayes' questions were forthright and business-oriented. It was almost as if Maryann had invited me so that I could provide information about the state of the business. But then I wondered why Maryann was acting like she was. In haste, fueled by discomfort and suspicion, I departed the house before the Hayes family returned.

Chapter 31 (December) – The Owner of the Ring

Since the catastrophic dinner at the Hayes residence, I attempted, with varying degrees of attempts, to divert my mind from the growing suspicion that Maryann had been taking advantage of me all along. Yet I could not ignore my doubts, as every moment that Maryann and I had together needed reexamination. I thought of that afternoon in the bookshop where I met her and the regard we shared. That memory seemed to consist of genuineness and lacked malicious intention. But then there were the words "*This may be an opportunity*" spoken by her mother when I first began to call on her. Those words made sense now, unfortunate sense. Moreover, they managed to seize many of our accounts, setting their rates well below our own. What better opportunity to draw away our trade was there than the one presented in using me to gain more details on the trade? As I contemplated all our shared moments, I began to regret ever trusting in someone else, as it proved to be a foolish and agonizing mistake. To my further dismay, I had to admit my mother's doubts had been justified all along.

Though my prospects with Maryann faltered as her family's designs against mine came to light, one thin thread of hope remained. I felt a deep conviction that if I could discover who owned the ring I might finally obtain something real in my life. As I left the house and headed towards the Revere shop, the air carried the bite of an early Boston winter, the kind that found its way underneath wool coats and numbed your fingertips. Dark grey smoke rose from brick chimneys, filling the air with the thick, bittersweet smell of burning wood. I strode towards the shop with the wind chilling my face, hurrying as though something was waiting for me.

When I arrived at the shop, I spotted Mr. Revere just as he was stepping out. If I hadn't been so swift, I might have missed him.

"Mr. Revere!" I called, walking hastily towards him.

He turned, and when he recognized me, he lifted his head slightly with a slight grin. "Mr. Thompson, come with me. I found something."

A sudden rush of energy coursed through me as I followed him into the shop. "What did you find?"

"I will show you. Hold on right here."

Mr. Revere went into the back, then came out with a ledger and a small box. He flipped the ledger open, turning the pages till he found the one he was looking for. He pointed to the page, and I leaned in to read its contents, my heart pounding as I scanned the words.

March 12th, 1799
Item: Signet ring, solid silver, oval bezel.
Design: Falcon in mid-stoop, talons outstretched toward prey.
Colors specified: Red.
Band: Plain, tapered.
Intended Recipient: *Abner Thorne.*

Delivered: June 26th, 1799 to Mr. Thorne.

With each line, my thrill dissolved, replaced by a sinking dread. I had the uneasy sense of trespassing into knowledge I was not meant to possess. Mr. Revere pulled the box over and opened it up, pulling out a piece of paper with a red wax seal on it.

"This is the wax impression used for the engraving," he said, handing it to me.

I held the paper in my trembling hand. The wax impression had a falcon stooping down to catch its prey, just as described. But seeing the engraving in a wax seal, with a name tied to it, rendered my father's journal entry and conversation with Mr. Pritchard palpable. I set the paper down and looked at Mr. Revere.

"Do you have an address?"

"While I trust you won't intend to do any harm with this information, I cannot divulge that," he said rather demandingly.

"This is enough. Thank you for your help."

As I exited, I wondered how I could obtain the address to the residence of Abner Thorne. Though I had found some answers, everything else seemed tangled and broken. Then there was a deep sense of doubt about the substance of what I was pursuing, as the family business was about to be sold while my courtship with Maryann was crumbling.

I hurried through the streets, driven by a restless mix of eagerness to discover more and the concern I would never find what I was looking for. Something told me my pursuit was important, but I couldn't explain why. On one hand, if I was able to find out where Abner Thorne was, maybe I could get the answers to why the indigo shipment was not picked up and possibly inquire more about his intentions. On the other stretched a void from which I might never escape, a darkness laden with perpetual failure.

Upon arriving at Mr. Hall's office, I knocked lightly and entered, where I found him intently reading at his desk.

"Caleb…what are you doing here?" he asked, straightening his posture.

"Do you know the name Abner Thorne?"

"Abner Thorne…Abner Thorne…hmmmm….ah, yes. That name is quite familiar…for a particular reason."

"What reason is that?"

"He was known to have fallen into financial ruin. Apparently, his creditors were furious after he piled up an unmanageable amount of debt and filed insolvency. Why do you ask?"

"Well, he may be the person who ordered the shipment that led my father to his conscription."

Mr. Hall's eyes widened. "Whoa! Slow down, Caleb. Are you suggesting he set your father up?"

"I suppose, in a way, yes. Possibly. I am not sure. I don't know what I am saying. I just know his family crest matches the ring my father described in his journal."

"Son, you cannot go around making these types of accusations. Why would he do such a thing?"

"I don't know. I just would like to find out if he ordered the shipment that was never picked up."

"You need to give me more details."

"Before my father departed on his last voyage, he signed a contract to purchase indigo for the New England Mercantile Co. Though no one seems to know of the New England Mercantile Co., or Mr. Prescott, who signed the contract, my father described this man in his journal as a wealthy man who wore a red family ring with a falcon on the crest. Mr. Revere confirmed the ring was made here in town."

"Abner Thorne does not deal with trade; that is one thing. He works as a struggling bookkeeper. Ask yourself, why would he be plotting to get your father conscripted? It's far-fetched."

My heart began to feverishly pump, as though I had a choice to make.

"You're the one person who I thought would gladly help. I don't have the words to describe my disappointment."

"Caleb, I am trying to help. This doesn't make sense."

"Well, maybe it will if I can track this Abner Thorne down."

I left Mr. Hall's office without another word. It was apparent that discussing the matter further with him would have done me no good. I had other avenues on how to obtain the information now that I knew Abner Thorne resided somewhere in town. Though I was angry at Mr. Hall, he did have a point. If Abner was not wealthy, where would he have gotten the silver used to pay upfront for the shipment, and what reason would he have to do such a thing?

I departed hastily towards the Green Dragon Tavern, entering the threshold I had passed through countless times before. I headed toward the tavernkeeper who knew everyone in town, where they lived, what they did for work, and the things they wanted to keep secret. He was standing as he usually would, waiting for the next thirsty soul to serve.

"Caleb, what can I get you?"

"I need help."

"Sure, what is it?"

"Have you heard the name Abner Thorne?"

"Thorne? Let me think," the tavernkeeper went into a deep thought, then said, "He used to frequent here, actually. But then, he got into a deep financial hole. Apparently, his fiancée left him before they could marry. He spent a winter in the Leverett Street almshouse after his insolvency. Apparently, he crawled out of poverty soon enough and now resides on Sheafe Street, I believe."

"Do you know which home he resides in?"

"That I do not know."

"I'm grateful for your help."

I left, heading towards Sheafe Street, passing creaking carts and merchants announcing their wares. When I arrived on Sheafe Street, there was little activity but candles filling the windows. The street was narrow and crooked, filled with mixed-sized houses, some wooden and small, while others were larger with federal-style brick facades. I walked up and down the street in the cold evening, impatient and wanting to find more answers, until a seafaring man in a thick faded wool coat exited a house.

"Excuse me, sir," I said as he came my way.

He slowed down and looked me dead in the eye. "What do you want? I'm in a hurry."

"I'm looking for Abner Thorne and was told he lived on this street."

The sailor stopped, looked around, then back to me.

"Abner lives in that house over there," he said, pointing to a crooked wooden house that leaned a little towards the alley as though it was about to come toppling down. "Best keep in mind, he's not the sort to welcome strangers at his door. Bit of an odd fish, keeps to himself and may be prone to being harsh."

"Thank you for the warning. Have a good day, sir."

The sailor quickly left and turned a corner. As for myself, I didn't linger. Maybe he was right. Maybe I was better off observing Abner before I began confronting him altogether. I left, planning to return during the day so I could see his coming and going while remaining discreet.

Chapter 32 (December) –
An Offer and Confessions

The following morning, Jameson informed me that Mr. Hall had paid us a visit that prior afternoon while I was out searching for answers.

"Mr. Hall was here yesterday. From what I heard, looks like somebody's offering to buy the business."

"Already? From whom?"

"I don't know. I heard him and Mother talking. They are apparently going to meet at the family office tomorrow to discuss more details."

Before I left for the day, I went into the parlor room, where I found an unsealed letter on the desk. I picked it up, and to my shock, the contents read:

To the Proprietors of the Atlantic Shipping Co.,

Having seen the posted advertisement in the *Boston Gazette* concerning the sale of your family's commercial enterprise, I write to express my interest in further discussing the particulars.

If agreeable to you, I would request the opportunity to examine the ledgers of the business and assets belonging to the enterprise at your earliest convenience.

You may leave a reply to the Standard Shipping Co. office.

Your humble and obedient servant,

Mr. Hayes

Each line dragged me downward until my heart seemed to sink entirely. With my mother already gone for the day, I assumed she was off responding to Mr. Hayes. All along, while my father's plight provided an opportunity, Maryann and her family were taking full advantage. That morning, I planned to visit Sheafe Street again. But now, I wanted to confront Maryann. The more I gave it thought, it was apparent attacking Maryann would not prevent the sale of the business. Frustrated and angered, I departed towards Sheafe Street. This time, hoping to discover exactly who Abner Thorne was.

The pale winter daylight covered Abner's old, crooked house as I waited for someone to step out. After waiting for who knows how long, observing men and women exit and enter their homes, from clerks to working poor, to merchants and tradesmen, finally, a man, in a top hat, with a white silk cravat exited Abner's home. Upon stepping into the street, his focus fell upon me. I turned my head aside at once, hoping he did not notice me watching. Though I could be seen a mile off as a stranger standing on the street looking from afar, Abner, in the top hat and fine dress, was no less noticeable. He continued east, turning the corner fast. I hurried to catch him, continuing to trail behind, staying far enough away so he could not notice me. As we weaved through the streets from

Salem Street to Cross Street, I wondered where he was heading. He seemed to be heading to an appointment, the way he stayed consistent with his pace. Keeping up was no easy task. I was caught between the need to stay near, yet unnoticed, while weaving through crowded streets.

Eventually, he came to State Street and turned towards Long Wharf. But when I caught up, I lost track of him amidst the busy street. I stumbled to the wharf and stopped, with my chest heaving, my breath casting white clouds into the air as I searched for him amidst the sea of people. Without any luck, I hurried onto the docks and slipped into the row of storehouses, climbing the stairs into the family counting room. There, I picked up my father's telescope and brought it close to my eye. My heart pounded like ocean water against the shore as I steadied my hands on the telescope, searching amongst the movements of the harbor. Then suddenly, I spotted Abner, in his top hat, walking towards India Wharf. He entered the counting houses that lined the newly constructed wharf. I continued searching, now surveying the gigantic new stone mass of India Wharf, its storefronts opening onto a broad cobbled stretch where cargo from Canton and Calcutta was unloaded each day. I continued to check every window for any movement. I spotted someone peering out a window on the first floor, but it appeared to be someone of a smaller stature than Abner. I continued to search, when I saw what appeared to be someone wearing a hat in the window of the second floor. Counting four windows from the right, I realized it was the same room I saw aglow the night my father's ship was set on fire. My heart pounded harder with every breath as my suspicions deepened.

After a long while, nothing else happened. I waited, looking out the window frequently, then sparingly, hoping something would catch my eye. I focused my attention on *Providence*, still anchored, unable to make any voyage, her mast damaged and her decks void of activity. Farther down the pier was a brig belonging to the Standard Shipping Co., readying for another journey to China, more riches to be accumulated.

As I continued looking out the window, I noticed a young woman, in a claret-colored gown walking towards the counting rooms at India Wharf. She was carrying documents that appeared to be quite important, as they were bundled and bound by a red ribbon. When I realized it was Maryann, my heart began to pump fervently again. I kept my eye on the building as she entered. I watched each window, waiting for her to appear. After a few quick moments, Maryann appeared in a room. I counted four windows from the right and on the second floor. She had entered the very room Abner Thorne had apparently entered, her claret gown clearly visible in the window. I wondered what she might have been doing there and what those documents were. A part of me didn't want to know. After a few moments, I saw her exiting, my telescope following every step as she walked away from the harbor.

Chapter 33 (December) – Confrontation at the Common

The next morning, I rushed to the Common, determined to find Maryann, as she frequented there often. My suspicions of her had grown, given the ties she apparently had with Abner Thorne. I stationed myself on a low stone boundary wall so that I could observe couples and the groups walking along the open field. As time passed, I lost count of the pairs of men and women, all seemingly adorned alike with top hats and with frock coats for the men and colorful gowns and head covering for the women, but no Maryann yet.

I sat brooding, anger burning, as I questioned whether her betrayal ran deeper than I had feared. To my astonishment, her carriage drew up, and with her stepped out Charles Derby. My anger went from a smolder to a full-fledged burning fire when I saw them step out together. Her invite to dinner was clear. She had no intention of progressing our courtship. Maryann, accompanied by Charles, strolled towards the large elm in the center, its summer canopy reduced to skeletal limbs. I quickly got up and walked over. Though she did not notice me at first, when she did, she froze, her eyes focusing on mine.

Charles was standing straight, his pretense exuberating, but I was indifferent to him. I walked towards her, breathing heavily, a tense scowl on my face.

"Caleb, what's wrong?"

"What's wrong?! Why would anything be wrong?!" I asked, hoping she might confess her misdeeds right away.

"Whoa! You need to respect our space, Caleb," Charles interjected, stepping forward with his hands half-raised, as though to stall me or perhaps to draw me into a fight.

"Charles, please give me a moment to converse with Caleb."

Charles gave me a long stare. Though I was now entertaining taking my anger out on him, I had to remain somewhat calm to get the answers I was seeking. He turned and walked away, not too far, so he could keep an eye on us.

"I'm sorry about the dinner."

"The dinner…ha…that's what you're sorry for!"

"Caleb, please!"

"What part of the dinner are you sorry about, exactly? The soup? Or the part where you were using me to gain information about my father's business?"

Her head tilted down, shaking. She looked at me, her head still down slightly. "What are you talking about?"

"Let me spell it out clearly. The dinner invitation was an opportunity to gather more information on the health of my family's business."

"That is not true!"

I held my eyes on her.

"Look, you're right, my father was prying. But…"

"But what?"

"It wasn't my idea! Why do you think I left the table? I told my father before the dinner to refrain from talking about your family's business."

"Then why invite me over?"

Maryann looked over to Charles, then back to me. "Because…I wanted to continue to see you."

"I'm sorry, I don't believe you. When I came to call on you for the very first time, I heard your mother say, 'This may be an opportunity.' And now I know what she meant."

Charles began to walk over towards us, but Maryann waved him off. Like an obedient pup, he went back to where he was waiting.

"Look. You are right. My mother wanted to use your pursuit of me as an advantage."

"And you went along."

"I know this sounds insane, but it was my opportunity to get to know you."

I stepped back, shaking my head. Maryann was admitting I had been right, yet the answers I truly sought gave me a deep sense of unease. "How do you know Abner Thorne?"

"What do you mean?"

"The man you met yesterday, Abner Thorne. What were you meeting him for?"

"You were following me?"

"Answer the question. How do you know each other?"

"He manages Mr. Payne's ledger and contracts. Why does it matter?"

"Honestly, I have no idea how deeply you, your father, or his partners are involved in the attacks on my family's business."

Maryann's brows furrowed. "Are you saying I had something to do with the fire on your father's ship?"

"Maybe?" I said, looking at her, searching for answers.

"This is nonsense! I am sorry if you think me false. But I acted from the pressure of duty to my family. At the same time, I wanted the chance to know you. Think about it: would I have quarreled with my own father at the table had I not cared for you?"

Her words made some sense, though I was still confused and angered.

"What else can you tell me about Abner Thorne?"

"I don't know him well enough. All I know is that he helps Mr. Payne with the ledgers and contracts. What is it about him you want to know?"

"It is quite a tale. Let me say only that I believe he keeps his share of secrets, and I intend to expose them."

She glanced over her shoulder, then back at me, lowering her voice. "I will admit, Mr. Thorne is quite odd. Still, I cannot shake the feeling there is something even more peculiar about Mr. Payne."

My eyes narrowed, wondering where she was going.

"He claims to have come to Boston from Marblehead, yet I cannot believe that to be true"

"I don't follow."

"I don't believe his family is from Marblehead, like he says they are. My aunt lives there. Has lived there all her life, in fact. Yet she's never heard of the Payne family."

I frowned. "Why would he lie about something like that?"

"I cannot say for certain. Yet there is something in him I do not trust."

I turned my collar up as the wind shifted, sending a cold gust our way. "I should go."

Maryann stepped closer, her eyes searching mine. "Please forgive me."

I held her gaze for a moment longer than I meant to. There were a dozen reasons to walk away, but none strong enough to make my feet move.

"I need to clear my mind," I said finally. "About all of it."

I left Maryann there, the cold wind tugging at the hem of my coat. The road stretched before me, uncaring and long. The air cut at my face, but it was nothing compared to the storm inside me. I wanted to hate her, but I couldn't. I wanted to forget her, but I didn't have the will. Yet now, there was Mr. Payne. What was he hiding? I was close to home, but I intended to take my time getting back. There was too much to unravel.

Chapter 34 (December) – Growing Suspicions

As the next day dragged on, with the need for more answers, I replayed my confrontation with Maryann over and over in my mind. I wanted to believe her. I wanted to believe that beneath the choreography of her mother's propriety and her father's ambition, there remained something untainted—something that belonged to us alone. But I pondered if her suspicions about Mr. Payne had been simply another well-placed distraction in the grand orchestration, just long enough to ensure my family's fall was irreversible. And yet, what if it wasn't?

The need for answers consumed me, leaving me unfit for anything else. So, I dressed quickly and made my way to Mr. Payne's shop at India Wharf. I wondered at my purpose as I walked along the wooden planks of the harbor. Was I chasing answers that would never present themselves?

I soon came to the India Wharf, the massive building of warehouses, offices, and stores, stretching long towards the sea. The edifice stood immense and orderly, its brick front marked by rows of windows set in strict symmetry. I found Mr. Payne's shop and entered. Porcelain teapots gleamed under shafts of morning sun. Bolts of silk from Macau were stacked with precision. Tea chests, each stamped with a foreign seal, were positioned at angles designed to catch the eye. And yet, something about the room was bare of warmth, as if no one had ever bothered to hang a painting or frame a family portrait. In every other merchant's office in town, there were relics, whether it was a faded silhouette portrait of a relative or a sketch of the ship that had brought the family fortune. But here, there was nothing. No past. Only commerce.

"Can I help you, sir?" asked a man who quickly came out from behind the counter. He wore a coat cut from fine black wool, its buttons trimmed in gold. His cravat was neatly folded, his breeches tucked perfectly into shoes polished to a high shine.

"I am merely observing your wares," I said.

"I remain at your service, should you have need."

He returned to his post, though glancing at me every so often. In the few minutes I stood there, at least five wealthy customers completed their purchases, each transaction conducted briskly, silver pieces of eight exchanged with cordial conversation. Mr. Payne's business was thriving. As I traced the edge of a porcelain vase, an idea took shape.

"Will Mr. Payne be in soon?" I asked, adopting the tone of a man with nothing but business on his mind. "I wondered if I might speak with him."

"He should be in shortly. May I ask the purpose of your inquiry?"

"My family owns a shipping company, and I thought there might be opportunities for us to work together."

The man, eager for commission or favor, led me to Mr. Payne's office. He extended his hand to the door and turned the knob.

"Please have a seat, Mr. Payne should be here any moment."

He kept the door open to let me know he was still present. The room was similarly unfriendly with just a desk and two chairs. No embellishments, no trophies of past success, no sign of the man himself. On the desk sat a copper miniature lockset, a silhouette portrait framed in delicate filigree. With no one around, I picked it up, opening it gently. The figure was of a woman. I examined it, turning it over and noted two curious details: the initials *E.S.* and the date *September 15, 1755.* I slowly set the portrait down, wondering who she could have been. Before I could turn the thought over in my mind, Mr. Payne appeared in the doorway.

His jaw was tight, his posture growing stiff. "Caleb. What brings you here?"

I quickly got out of my chair and stood. "I was hoping we could discuss business."

He laughed, a dry sound devoid of humor, and crossed the room to his desk. Before sitting, he placed the portrait into his pocket looking at me intently.

"Business? With the *Atlantic Shipping Company*?" He let the name hang in the air like a punchline. "That's bold, given the circumstances."

"Circumstances change," I said. "Especially when one knows the right people."

"I suppose they do," he replied, then looked at me with a thin smile.

I could see his hand resting briefly over his pocket, as though to find comfort from the silhouette out of view.

"So, tell me," he said, leaning back, "what is this really about?"

"I was serious," I said. "I'm considering clients beyond Boston, and I figured you might have insight, particularly in Marblehead."

"Marblehead?" he repeated, the word coming slower than necessary. "Why not stay local?"

"Well, we know the circumstances I have locally."

"Ah, yes. I'll have to think about it," he said, though his expression suggested no such intention. "And forgive my confusion, but why ask me?"

Before I could reply, the man from the counter appeared at the door.

"Before I forget, I have some letters here for you."

"Come in."

He walked over and passed the letters onto the desk. "Excuse me for interrupting."

"No need to apologize. We were just having an entertaining conversation between two acquaintances," Mr. Payne said, looking at me with a slight grin.

"Oh. Do you know each other?"

"Well, I wouldn't say we know each other. More like know of. This is Caleb Thompson of the Atlantic Shipping Company."

The man's chin rose as he took a long look at me. I stood up, sensing that whatever pretense I'd arrived with had run its course. I took a long look at Mr. Payne. He was not himself. Not that I knew the man well enough, but he seemed off, nervous.

"I can come back another time." I turned and walked towards the door.

"I have a sneaky suspicion you are up to something, Caleb."

Blood rushed to my face. I turned to leave before my temper got the better of me, and I gave away my true intention. Before I could exit the shop, the front door swiftly opened. Abner in his top hat stood in front of me, nearly colliding with me at the threshold. His expression was cold and threatening as he held the knob. A heavy signet ring gleamed on his finger, its red gemstone catching my eye with every movement. I gave a slight nod and studied him closely, imprinting every detail: the rigid line of his square jaw, the deep shadows beneath his eyes, and the peculiar way he held himself. He nearly pushed me aside and continued towards the back office.

I stepped outside with aim, to get away as fast as I could while my thoughts circled like a ship caught in a gale. Bewilderment pursued me as I walked away from the wharf. I couldn't believe what I just saw—the signet ring! Then there was the portrait with the initials: *E.S.* Those very initials matched the carving upon the headstone of the woman lost in the fire. Coincidence, maybe. But the day of birth matched as well. Suddenly, the white roses Mr. Payne held at the Hayes residence made unfortunate sense. They were the same type left at the grave! The coincidences were too precise to be mere coincidence. My pulse beat rapidly and my breath shortened between intervals. There was an account here, one buried beneath decades of silence and soot. I had come to Mr. Payne's door seeking answers. What I discovered was something far more dangerous.

Chapter 35 (December) – A Secret Meeting

All at once, the pieces clicked into place from the portrait of the woman and Maryann's doubts about Mr. Payne's Marblehead origins, revealing a far darker reality than I'd imagined. It was, I'll confess, terrifying. Yet amid the impenetrable gloom of it all, Maryann's notion extended a beacon of hope and helped me to unlock the answers I had been searching for all along. That evening, I penned a letter to her, offering my forgiveness and forewarning.

Dear Maryann,

I write to you now to offer my unreserved forgiveness. However, I have unearthed a troubling and significant truth about Mr. Payne. A truth too complex and dark to set to parchment, given its implications for his standing with your father.

Would you grant me a meeting in private so we can speak freely? Will you meet me at the marketplace tomorrow at noon, alone? Meet me in the alleyway towards the back of the marketplace on Market Square.

Yours sincerely,
Caleb Thompson

I slipped the folded note into an envelope, nestled it within a hymnbook, and set off for Maryann's home. By the time I reached the Hayes residence, my nerves began to shake like a leaf. Both of her parents were home. But more concerning was that candles flickered in Mr. Payne's windows. I raised my hand to knock. The door swung open before I could summon courage. Mr. Hayes stood on the stoop, his expression as austere as carved marble. His gaze pinned me in place. "One moment," he said and disappeared into the house.

While I stood at the threshold, I could see a figure standing in the window next door. When I realized it was Mr. Payne watching, my heart beat hard, my nerves faltering every moment he lingered.

Then a moment later, Maryann appeared, her face softly lined with concern. "Caleb…" she murmured.

"Good evening," I managed. "I brought this." I offered her the hymnbook.

She accepted it with a graceful nod. "Thank you."

"There's a letter inside," I said, my voice low. "Please read it tonight."

She hesitated on the threshold. "Would you like to come in?"

I shook my head. "I fear it's too much for tonight. When you've read it, send a message if you cannot meet me tomorrow."

"Are you in jeopardy?"

"Yes, but please promise me you will read the letter. I must take my leave."

A small, understanding smile flickered across her lips as she closed the door gently. For a moment, I stood in the dim glow of the oil lamps, knowing once she unfolded those pages, everything would change for her, for me, and for the growing suspicions gathering around Mr. Payne and his associate, Abner Thorne.

The following day, I made my way to the loud and bustling market, a perfect cover for Maryann and me to speak in private. I took my place in the alley where I asked her to meet and felt time stretch with every passing moment. Eventually, Maryann did show.

"I cannot stay long. I managed to buy some time away from Mr. Boyle."

"Have you read the note?"

She glanced toward the street where she came from. "I did. Thank you for forgiving me. I wouldn't know what I would have done if you had not." She paused and looked around. "What is this grave matter regarding Mr. Payne?"

"Much requires explanation. So please, listen to what I have to say."

She nodded.

"Your intuition was correct. He is not from Marblehead. He is from Boston!"

"I knew he wasn't from there. How did you find out?"

"Well, I went to his shop."

"You went to his shop? How did that go?"

"What I discovered is quite alarming. He did not tell me outright, of course. But the lockset on his desk told me everything."

"A lockset?"

"Yes. He had a portrait miniature lockset of what I believe was his mother."

Maryann said not a word. I was not sure if she was following me or if I should stop at this moment.

"Go on."

"The initials on the lockset match the name and birthdate of a woman from Boston."

"That is odd. How do you know all this?"

"What follows is of a darker nature. His mother burned in a fire after the Revolutionary War."

"Oh my! That is terrible!"

"A mob burned down his family house after the war. His mother and father perished in the fire. They had a son."

"He is the son who survived?"

"Unfortunatley, yes. And I believe he set up my father to be conscripted."

At this moment, a few townspeople passed and looked our way. We nodded so they would not think scandalously of us, yet we did anticipate rumors about our supposed impropriety to circle.

"Listen, I know this sounds insane. But there is so much more. You know those flowers you have been giving him?"

"Yes…what about them?"

"I saw the same flowers on the graves of his mother and father here in town."

Maryann shook her head. "But what does this have to do with your father?"

"During the war, my father was gathering lists of suspected loyalists who supported the Crown. His father was on the list. My father divulged this information to his friend. It got out and then the fire."

Maryann raised her hands to her face in shock. Then she said, "you need to go to the constable!"

"I plan to. That is why I asked to meet you. This will have severe consequences for your father's business."

Maryann paused, pondering the implications. "Of course. But, Caleb, this is more important, as tragic as it is. I have no words to express. The sorrow. I am sorry you had to learn about all this. If in fact there are consequences, then so be it."

"I will let you know what the constable says."

"Please do. And keep safe."

Maryann left the alleyway; then so did I. Though I was relieved that she believed me, doubt crept in. If justice was served, then her father's business would suffer and who knew what would become of us.

The following morning, I made my way to the North Watch House at the dock on Long Wharf. A biting chill filled the air as clouds massed over the harbor, deepening an already shadowy day. I rehearsed what I would tell the port watchman numerous times. I was confident I would convince him to look into the matter more, if not make an immediate arrest. When I reached his station, I found him in his usual mood.

"What complaints do you have on such a pleasant December morn'?"

"I need to have a word with you. I believe I know who set the fire on my father's ship."

He perked up, mostly from wanting to be entertained on a cold winter day than to listen with curiosity.

"Well, then go ahead."

I spilled my theory before him, every word tumbling out in a rush.

The watchman, accustomed to madmen, unruly sailors, and drunkards, listened with the impassivity of a man waiting for a small storm to pass. After I finished, he stood there contemplating, almost as if I laid out a substantial case rather than losing my mind. Then he broke his silence.

"You need more than that," he said finally. "Something solid. Something undeniable."

I couldn't believe what he was saying. The contempt I had for the man grew, almost uncontrollable.

"But do you even see what I am saying?"

He shook his head. "To be honest, Caleb, it doesn't matter what I believe. It matters what facts and evidence you have. If you want to convince the constable, you will need more than just what you believe."

"I can show you the graves! And the ring! From Abner Thorne, it matches the description in my father's journal. I witnessed this with my own eyes!"

The watchman switched from casual indifference to becoming agitated. "If I were you, I would change course. Go home!"

But home no longer felt like an option. I wandered the streets, revisiting every detail in my mind, fitting the pieces together until the picture was unmistakable. My family was about to lose everything. I was about to become nothing. And unless I could find a way to expose the truth, to prove what I knew in my bones, the story of the Thompson family would end not with triumph but with a footnote. I went on my way, the watchman's response sharper than the December air.

Chapter 36 (December) – A Somber Christmas Holiday

A few days later, the family gathered for our customary Christmas Eve dinner. It was a ritual that, under ordinary circumstances, provided a brief reprieve from the hardships endured during the year. The table was set with what few luxuries remained: a tureen of oyster stew, a modest roast, and cider. The candles flickered against the paneled walls, their reflection visible in the window glass, while outside, the wind whispered through the alleys, rattling the shutters like someone too polite to knock hard.

My mood was one of quiet perseverance. Beneath the veneer of observing the holiday, my mind churned with my theory though the rejection from the watchman still stung. For now, there was no chance I would divulge what I held inside with my family as they shared some semblance of peace.

Mother came to the table, her countenance stoic.

"I want you all to know that the sale of the family business had been agreed upon. I'm signing the papers next week."

"Where will we go, Mother?" Alice asked.

"We will sell the house and move closer to your relatives in Satucket."

"Satucket?" Jameson replied. "I'm staying here in Boston. Once my leg is fully recovered, I will go back to work."

"Then the family won't be together," Alice replied.

"What about you, brother?" Jameson asked.

Jameson's question was sincere. Though I had caused him grief, he still wanted to remain near me. "I don't know what I will do. I will need to contemplate it more."

Jameson sank into his chair.

"You will need to come to a conclusion, Caleb, as time is running out," my mother reminded me.

Time was surely running out. For more than one reason or the other.

"I think this is a good thing for the family. We will be able to start anew," Charlotte said, though everyone knew she was aiming to please Mother.

Afterall, moving away from Boston, seemed to surrender much more than the town but on what was anchoring us all—the family. In short order, we began to eat in silence, pondering what the future may hold.

On Christmas morning at Old North Church, I sat alone in our family pew, while my family and the rest of the community exchanged warm messages. The bells rang out over the rooftops, their reverberations echoing through the streets of Boston and through my unsettled mind. Maryann and her family were towards the front of the church near their pew. Every once in a while, she would glance over my way. But there was a mass of people between us feverishly speaking to one another and little room to maneuver through.

As the congregation gathered into their pews and seats, the pastor called for prayer. I sat drooped into the bench of the pew, my hands folded, my lips silent. Every moment of silence was the echo of failure. It was the kind of morning meant for tradition: the quiet unfolding of familiar rituals, where hymns were sung with more zeal and where the cold was kept at bay by the comfort of togetherness. As for me, this day would not adhere to tradition. I had spent the last few days fitting together pieces that shouldn't have fit at all: flowers on a gravestone, a portrait bearing the same name, the convenient story of Mr. Payne's origins, the signet ring on the hand of his associate, and the entries in my father's journals. Each piece by itself was a peculiarity. But together, they formed a grim picture of lies and revenge. Still, the watchman did not accept my theory. And if I gained no new convincing facts to present, injustice would prevail.

After the service, as families exchanged greetings and filed out into the cold, Maryann came over to our family pew, her gloved hands clasped before her, her face half-lit by the morning sun. I wondered what she had thought since I revealed my theory about Mr. Payne.

"Merry Christmas, Caleb," she said.

"Merry Christmas," I replied, though my voice held none of the sentiment.

"How did the conversation go with the watchman?" she asked, her eyes drifting towards where her parents stood.

"He rejected what I had to say, that…that," I restrained myself, aware of who was surrounding me and where I was.

"Did he say he would look into the matter at all?"

"No. In fact, he told me to change course."

"Could you gather more evidence?"

"What other evidence can I obtain? Without a confession, which we both know will never come, I don't know what else I can do," I said despairingly.

"I have something to tell you."

"Of course," I said, wondering why Maryann was acting so serious.

"I wanted you to know that I declined Charles' proposal to marry him."

"What? How did your parents feel about this?" I said quietly.

"They thought it was a mistake."

Her words saddened me. It wasn't a surprise that her parents preferred Charles over me. But now I felt their rejection.

"We will be having a New Year's gathering. We would welcome your presence there."

For a moment, I forgot all the pain, all the sorrow I had felt. Maryann had rejected Charles Derby and invited me to her home. It was all too good to be true. I contemplated her invitation. Then my moment of joy was quelled by the thought of her parents' preferences and the unfortunate ties Mr. Payne had to her father's business.

"Will Mr. Payne be there?"

"I believe he will be. I haven't mentioned anything to my father yet. But I can?"

"What good will it do? I have only theories, conjecture. I will appear as though I have gone mad. Given your parents' apparent preferences, I think that would destroy our courtship."

"My parents will come around. They just need to understand you better. I would still like to see you; will you come?"

I hesitated. The thought of Mr. Payne being present at the home stirred up an anger so fierce within me that I became scared of what I might do.

"I believe so, yes," I replied, still unconvinced I could go and avoid making a fool of myself by confronting Mr. Payne, or worse.

I left the church and walked back towards home full of mixed emotion; elated about my mending courtship with Maryann, indecisive about her offer, and heavy-hearted about the looming situation regarding Mr. Payne. That night, I lay awake as the hours crept past, the moonlight in the windows shining a dull glow on the floor. Though my family's future was bleak, my own was beginning to take shape depending on which paths I took. I had been offered a glimmer of hope: a chance to rebuild and to be with the girl I have set my affections upon. And yet, sleep would not come.

I played out the sequences. If I were to explain this all to Maryann's father when I had the right moment, maybe I could convince him to end his business relations with Mr. Payne. Even if it came to that, Mr. Payne would not leave town quietly. And that was assuming Mr. Hayes would believe me. The thrill and hope of it all began to dwindle as I thought about it more. Then as I considered what would become of my family as they left Boston, I became even more desperate. I grew anxious as I thought about their fate whether it be a life of struggle and poverty.

I spent the rest of the night between the thought of building on what Maryann and I had and the weight of loyalty and honor. I began to see things more clearly as I replayed all the events that took place over the course of the year within my mind. From the early news of my father's disappearance, I set out to find the truth. But yet my motives for maintaining the family business and carrying out his legacy were unfortunately driven by selfishness. I wanted to impress Maryann. Along the way, as I found out more about my father, I learned more about myself. For all my father's faults, his harshness, his impossible expectations, the years I wasted resenting him—he had given me something intangible. With my bitterness resigned, it became clear he had given me fortitude and a legacy of virtues to follow. Virtues that were meant to last beyond his life. And that was not mine to abandon.

Chapter 37 (December/January) – Two Front Doors

On the afternoon of New Year's Eve, heavy snow had begun to fall upon the streets. Each snowflake seemed to drift more slowly than the last, as if nature itself were reluctant to turn the final page of the year. In neighboring households, fires were being stoked, candles lit, glasses raised to the hopeful promises of a new year with reflections on the past. At the Hayes residence, a grand celebration would soon be taking place. As for the Thompsons, there was no such appetite for that. Each member of the family remained isolated from one another. At least in spirit. My mother remained in her bedroom putting her personal belongings away into a pine chest, readying for our immediate move. My sisters performed chores around the house in silence, while Jameson lay in bed, still recovering from his injury.

As for myself, I spent much of the day waiting for the sun to set. I stared out the window, watching the snow gather on the sills, wondering if I had imagined everything that had drawn me to this precipice. On my bed lay my father's instruments, which he used for his work as a spy, and his pistol. For a moment, I wavered, considering doing nothing at all. Perhaps, attending the party was the best option; I could drink some ale, then offer half-hearted toasts, and convince myself that the past was past.

As dusk fell, I threw on my father's coat and stepped into the streets blanketed with snow. The town had quieted with the usual bustle, and oil-lit lamps were being lit by lamplighters. Maryann's home was bright while people stepped into the home for the gathering. Mr. Payne's house was much dimmer, lit by only a few candles flickering in the windows. I waited in the shadow of a neighboring building, watching until he emerged, fastening his cloak beneath his chin and stepping out to enter Hayes residence.

This was my opportunity.

The storm concealed my presence, the snow swallowing my footsteps as I approached the federal-style townhouse. But as I got near, one of Maryann's friends spotted me.

"Caleb! Are you joining the celebration?"

"I was planning to stop by, yes," I replied.

I waited for her friend to enter. I wondered if I just brought attention to myself and how it would play out. Surely, she would be telling Maryann she saw me outside. Then who else would end up knowing I was around?

When there was no one else to be seen, I hurried and went around the back to the side of Mr. Payne's townhome. Before me was a six-foot brick wall. I ran and leaped, grabbing hold of the ragged edge, then slowly pulled myself up to the top. Remaining on my chest, I slowly dangled myself on the other side. I let go, dropping into his backyard, fenced in by a brick wall. I heard a watchman patrol ringing out on Beacon Street, reminding me, if caught, I would be in serious trouble. I peered in one of the windows, my breath fogging the glass. I stood, trembling but resolute. This was no time for hesitation, so I began to pick the box lock on the back door with a filed-down key. But the lock was harder to pick than I expected; the tumblers resisted like they had been waiting for me. Sweat traced its way down my back despite the chill. With a final twist, the lock opened, and I removed it. Twisting the knob, the door creaked open into a surreal quietness as if the house itself were holding its breath.

Inside, the air was biting with cold, the hearth empty and dark. Carefully as I stepped, the floorboards creaked with each movement. However, the chatter from the energetic crowd at the Hayes residence masked any noise I made.

I carefully walked up the stairs and entered his bedroom. It was furnished with just a bed and a wardrobe. I opened the wardrobe slowly so as not to disturb, his clothes neatly lined and organized. But nothing of interest was found. I could hear the laughter through the walls, and it saddened me. Maryann was most likely anticipating my arrival, yet I was not there.

I continued down the stairs to his office. There was a desk and a bookshelf. The desk was organized with an inkwell, a quill pen, a stack of parchment, a wax seal kit, and nothing else. Like his shop, the walls were unadorned: less the office of a man proud of his work and more the space of someone with a singular focus on building wealth or something more sinister. My hands shook as I opened the first drawer. There were papers and ledgers neatly stacked. Among the papers was a deed to a house. I studied the address: *43 Winter St, Boston, MA*. My father had never mentioned the Smiths by name. But there it was: cold proof that Mr. Payne was tied to them and the fire. I folded the deed carefully and set it on the floor as my heart pounded profusely.

I opened the ledger next, flipping through page after page of neatly transcribed transactions. Porcelain. Silk. Tea. I flipped farther back until I reached a page dated near the time of my father's final voyage: a withdrawal for forty silver ounces! No explanation. No corresponding entry.

Then came a loud raucous and murmuring through the walls. Though I had discovered proof of a motive, I thought twice about my choice. I felt the emptiness that Charles must have felt when he was rejected, pondering if I was about to lose Maryann as well because of what I was doing. I turned to the bookshelf, my hands moving faster now, foreboding overriding care. I found a slim leather journal between a row of account books. I grabbed it and sat down on the cold wooden floor. When I opened it, a folded letter slipped out. Its contents read:

Mr. Payne,

The conscription has been completed. Payment in full is required. Meet at Long Wharf on the 12th of June, 1805. A man by the name of Reinald Ashfor will meet you for the payment. —Captain Rotheram

My stomach twisted as I recognized the name of the captain that was detailed in my father's journal. I had solid proof now! I carefully placed the letter into my coat. *Conscription.* A word I had not been familiar with before was now etched into my memory never to be forgotten.

Fearing its contents, there was something fiendish about the journal that made me think twice about reading it. I already had the proof I needed and I had already been in the home for a while. But this was my only chance to find out what lay inside, so I flipped through his journal stopping on entries that caught my attention:

June 7th, 1796

Nearly a decade has passed since my father and mother perished in a deadly fire. I have tried to bury the memory of the home set ablaze by an unruly and evil mob. But I cannot forget. The bitterness inside of me not only remains, it grows.

December 24th, 1799

Ten days ago, George Washington was declared dead and it pleases me.

February 13th, 1804

Today I have learned the name of the man who was responsible for the death of my parents. The mob that killed my parents in cold blood was informed by someone who made it known that my father was a Loyalist. This man, Benjamin Thompson, apparently worked for Geroge Washington as a spy. I am a step closer to avenging their deaths.

March 3rd, 1804

I have found where Mr. Thompson lives.

In terror, I looked away from the journal. Before I could read further, the front door flung open with a loud bang, followed by someone shouting from the bottom floor.

"Who's in there?" a voice called loudly.

I froze, thinking of what to do. Then I quickly scrambled to exit the room, realizing I forgot to grab the journal. But whoever was below was approaching fast. I bolted to the secondary set of stairs, their purpose for servants, and tumbled down to the basement floor. I heard someone coming back down the main stairs as I quickly exited the back door. I climbed the brick wall again, scraping my arms against the porous brick. I dropped onto the back street into the snow and ran without looking back.

"Stop! Thief!!" Mr. Payne yelled.

Behind me was the sound of pursuit: the crunch of boots and the shouts from Mr. Payne. I kept running, weaving through alleys, the snow blinding in its fury. I continued until the footsteps behind me were no longer. I headed back towards home, glancing around to see if anyone was still following. But all I could see were the tracks I'd left. I kept walking, trying to catch my breath, my lungs burning from the freezing air. I was only a few blocks from home when I cut through an alleyway. But there, at the other end, stood Mr. Payne. I quickly turned around when his associate, Abner, tackled me into a drift, my face pressing into the freezing, gritty road. Luckily, I twisted free and quickly rose to my feet as Mr. Payne approached me fast, trapping me in the narrow alley.

"Your father got what he deserved," he spat.

"He didn't set that fire!"

"My parents were murdered!"

With a rush of frantic alarm, I quickly reached into my coat and pulled out my father's pistol. I cocked it and aimed at Mr. Payne's chest, wrapping my finger around the trigger.

"You wouldn't," said Abner.

"You know your father deserved what came to him," Mr. Payne said, daring me to pull the trigger.

I aimed the pistol steadily, both hands trembling, coupling the trigger. Then, in sudden resolve, I discharged the pistol into the night's sky. The shot echoed loudly through the empty passageway. Without hesitation, they rushed me. Fists met ribs; boots met my face, the cold cutting into every open space. They rummaged through my coat, searching, but I had pinned the letter between my arm and side, holding onto it as though my life depended on it.

"What are you all doing down there!?" came a voice from a nearby window.

A neighbor! Exactly what I was hoping for.

Mr. Payne straightened, smoothing his coat, while I stood hunched, blood dripping from my mouth.

"He broke into my home!"

Then a group of men approached; a watchman showed up along with other men of the watch, including the port watchman. The port watchman grabbed and pulled me back while the others detained Mr. Payne and Abner.

"What were you doing, Caleb?"

My pulse continued to race, my breathing deep and fast. I couldn't believe I was caught.

"These two men were attacking this young man."

"He broke into my home! And he fired a pistol."

"Is that true? Where's the pistol?" the watchman asked, still gripping me tightly.

One of the watchmen scanned the snow-covered ground, found it, and dangled it to be seen.

"Mr. Payne is responsible for my father's death!" I exclaimed, struggling to gain some space from the watchman's hold.

"This is absurd; he is lying!".

"I have the proof! There is a letter in my coat!"

The watchman searched my coat and found the letter. He held the letter and renewed his tight grasp on me.

"All three of you are coming with us."

Mr. Payne's face twisted in fury as the watchmen held tightly onto him.

"No one will believe you," he said as the watchmen forced us toward the Boston Gaol.

Shock entered my body the moment we arrived at the gaol. Though centered amidst public life, it was clearly a fortress of stone meant to keep those inside separated from society in more ways than physically. We entered through a heavy wooden door bound in blackened iron, stepping into the dingy interior. The air was damp and fetid, thick with the stench of mildew, straw, and rot. The barred windows carried with it cold, creeping drafts. We were separated into different cellrooms, with Mr. Payne and Abner in with the petty criminals and me in with the crowd of men who had committed unspeakable crimes from murders who were awaiting executions to arsonists who had destroyed property.

"Why am I being thrown in here?"

"We can't put you all together, of course." The jailor closed the wooden door behind me, leaving me to fend for myself with the most ungodly of men.

I had no intention of making conversation, withdrawing myself from the prisoners like prey from its predators. Moments passed slowly, the cold room and isolation I felt bringing me to deep despair. My thoughts began to entertain the punishment I would receive. Would I be publicly beaten? I imagined the guests at the Hayes residence, once celebrating a new year, now discussing what had just occurred as word was undoubtedly spreading fast. Then a deeper dread entered my soul as I thought about my undoubtedly shattered future with Maryann. Hour by hour, the night crawled as hopelessness kept me company.

"He is scared," one of the prisoners taunted, prompting the rest to burst out with unified cackling.

Worse yet, it was becoming apparent that sooner or later, I was going to have to fend for myself.

After a long while, as I sat on the cold ground, heavy footsteps and the jangle of keys caught our attention.

Then a loud, deep voice called out. "Caleb Thompson! Come to the door!"

I quickly gathered myself and walked past the men eagerly waiting to test me more. When I got to the door, it slowly opened revealing a jailer standing in front of me, his angry countenance glaring at me.

"You are at liberty to walk."

I exited the cell, puzzled by my sudden fortune. The port watchman, ironically a welcoming face, stood in the dim hallway.

"Come with me!"

As we passed the cell where Mr. Payne was held, relief entered my body.

The port watchman escorted me out of the gaol and into the cold snowy night. He held up the letter.

"Breaking and entering is no small crime. But this…this is a much more serious matter," he said. "You are lucky to have Mr. Hall's help in corroborating your story."

Outside of the jail stood my mother, her worried face beneath her bonnet focused on me. Beside her was Mr. Hall.

I looked at the port watchman. Though I would not have considered him a friend, I still thanked him then walked towards my mother and Mr. Hall.

My mother came towards me, embracing my cold body. I hugged her back tightly.

"Caleb," she said. "I am sorry for how I treated you with my unkind words."

"It's all right, Mother. You weren't wrong. I was selfish."

She hugged me again, tighter this time, sobbing. "Your father would have been proud," she said, looking at me.

She let me go.

I had a long look at Mr. Hall, my heart warmed by his presence. "Thank you for helping me."

"Of course, Caleb. When your mother informed me about this, I had no other choice. I am sorry I doubted you."

"No harm done. I understand. What do you think will happen to Mr. Payne?"

"Right now, he is charged with assault and disorderly conduct. However, the investigation into this matter will continue," Mr. Hall replied.

"I can't believe he went that far."

"He betrayed everything his family stood for, Caleb," Mr. Hall replied.

The snow continued to fall as we made our way towards Kilby Street. The road ahead would be long and filled with no small measure of courage and will. But at last, we were walking toward truth rather than from it.

Chapter 38 (January) –
A New Beginning

After the chaotic events of New Year's Eve, I concluded my way of seeing the world would never be the same. The port watchman paid us a visit to inform us that Abner Thorne confessed to setting the fire to *Providence* under Mr. Payne's direction. Apparently, Abner was being paid handsomely to do Mr. Payne's bidding but not enough to take the fall.

The watchman, unapologetic about his false accusations towards me, reiterated that he was simply performing his duty. He reminded me that what I did under normal circumstances would have led to severe consequences and shame. He did, however, extend a small token of sympathy, giving me the most recent copy of the *Boston Gazette*. An article about the incident was printed, detailing the events of Dameron Payne's thirst for revenge and revealing his actual name, Samuel Smith. There was also a section that portrayed me as someone who was being faithful to my family, though there was an emphasis on respecting property. As for my father, the rumors about his loyalty to the Crown were finally put to rest. Agreed to by my mother, the article detailed his work as a spy for Washington—and that made me delighted.

Clearing up who caused the fire also brought immediate relief to the family business: the insurance claim could proceed, and we began to rebuild *Providence*. Though many of the broken pieces had been mended, the sale of the family business loomed. As the week passed, there was a quiet, suspended unease stationed in me, as I hadn't heard from Maryann yet.

On the day before the papers were to be signed, I resigned myself to the docks, where *Providence* was beginning to be repaired by carpenters. I was disheartened by the eventual transfer of the family business into the hands of the Standard Shipping Co., consigning my father's legacy to a memory. When the day turned to evening, I headed back home. The sun had set, and I wondered what I would do when the sale took place.

While in the parlor room, soon after evening had fallen, I heard a knock on the door.

"Caleb, could you get the door?" my mother requested from her bedroom.

Her request was quite peculiar. Even stranger was that she was seemingly content all day as she sat quietly in her room reading. I would have preferred that she be the person to welcome the guest, most likely the person responding to the sale of our home. But I did not argue. I got up and walked towards the door. When I opened it, I was stunned by who stood there. It was not Mr. Hayes who stood there at the threshold or a potential buyer of our home. It was Maryann, with her magnificent red hair and friendly countenance.

"Come with me," she said, her cheeks rosy pink from the cold.

"Where are we going?"

"You'll see."

I doubted if I was ever going to see her again, and here she was standing in front of me, asking me to go with her. She offered her hand, which I took without hesitation. We climbed into the carriage; then Mr. Boyle snapped the reins. We passed familiar storefronts and faces I had long recognized, yet the world about me felt altered, oddly unfamiliar. When we arrived at Old North Church, confusion set in.

"The church?" I asked.

"Stop asking questions," she said.

I exited the carriage with Maryann soon after. She led me to the front door, where inside, a caretaker greeted us. He handed us lanterns, my curiosity piquing as I wondered why Maryann had taken me here. The sanctuary was empty, the air heavy with the scent of aging wood and a faint smell of whale's oil. She led me to a narrow door near the rear, a door I had never noticed before. She began climbing the steep wooden staircase, lantern in hand. I followed, the steps groaning beneath my weight as I ascended, the air growing cooler and thinner with each flight.

The stairway twisted and turned, becoming narrower with each landing. We passed the great wheels that turned the bells, their spokes worn smooth by decades of motion. With my lantern held before me, I thought of Captain John Pulling, Jr. and Robert Newman, who once trod this same path to signal the British approach.

"Up there," she said, nodding toward a final ladder that vanished into darkness.

I climbed first, the rungs cold beneath my hands. At the top, I emerged onto the steeple, where the light blue winter sky unfolded above us in a panorama of flickering stars. We set the lanterns down and came to the railed edge overlooking the town. From this height, the town looked majestic. The streets, glazed with snow, gleamed under the streetlamps. Windows glimmered with candles, and beyond the rooftops, the harbor lay quiet with ships that glowed from lantern light, bobbing in their berths like floating hearths.

"Isn't it wonderful?" Maryann asked, standing beside me.

"It's incredible," I replied, pausing for a long look out towards the ocean. "How did you get access to the steeple?"

"I asked the pastor for a favor. As you know, my parents made a rather generous donation to the steeple's repair. There are certain benefits to being a Hayes."

Maryann remained reserved and quiet while we stood overlooking the view of the town.

"When I was sitting in the dingy gaol, I wondered if I would ever see you again."

"You scared me," she said softly. "There were moments I thought what we had would be lost for good. Don't ever think of doing that again," she said with a slight smirk.

"I don't plan on it."

She turned to face me. "My father has a proposal."

"Your father?"

"A joint venture."

"A partnership?"

"Yes," she said, offering me a slow, inviting smile. "You know the ledgers. You know the routes. You know the competition," she said tilting her head. "The Atlantic Shipping Company and the Standard Shipping Co. working together."

I drew in a slow breath, stunned by the enormity of her words. "What made your father agree to this?"

"I admit, it took him a moment…well, several *moments*…to process everything. Between you breaking into someone's home, Mr. Payne's real identity, his family's tragedy, and the elaborate scheme of revenge he executed."

"Whoes idea was this?"

"We had a long talk, and it became apparent this was the right way forward."

"So then, this was your persuasive abilities at play here?"

"In the end, my father recognized your devoted heart to yours. And he knew I wanted to continue our courtship. But there are a few conditions."

"Please proceed."

"One, no gambling. Two, no strong spirits."

"Well, then, how do we get started?"

Maryann came close to me, the scent of her lavender soap mingling with the cold air. Before I could say anything, she leaned in and kissed me. Standing high above the candlelit town with Maryann by my side, the family business salvaged, all my father's ghosts laid to rest, I knew: every risk I had taken to honor my father, every chance moment between Maryann and me had led me to this moment. And it was worth the wager.

Q & A With Author Asher Clark

Question: *What inspired you to write this story?*

Answer: It grew from an idea about a coming-of-age idea and curiosity of how life was after the Revolutionary War. It's a time period where little is written about. A lot was going on around the time of this novel from George Washington's passing, to the Napoleonic War and eventual 2nd war with Britain. The 2nd generation of Americans had a lot to contend with!

Question: *How difficult was writing a historical fiction novel?*

Answer: Historical fiction is fun, but also challenging. Especially, when it comes to this time period since there is a lot of digging to do! You want to be accurate to the time period but also be able to have the creativity and imagination that makes a story exciting to read.

Question: *Do you have plans to write more?*

Answer: I do in fact. I have a detective series I am working on that is set right after the Revolutionary War, involving a sleuth that is a former Washington Spy. I also am working on a Sci-Fi series revolving around AI.

Question: *Can you see this ever becoming a movie?*

Answer: It would be a dream if it ever did. The story has a lot of elements where if it were told visually it could be epic! From the Boston Harbor scenes, historical taverns, the inside of grand federal-style homes, this would be a fun movie. And don't forget the historical Boston part of it!

Question: *How can readers support the author?*

Answer: If you'd like to help, leaving a review on Amazon is one of the most powerful things you can do. Reviews help other readers decide whether to take the plunge, and I'd be truly grateful for your words.

Question: *How can I follow you for more of your writing?*

Answer: If you so kindly would want to continue following there are few ways.

I am on Instagram: @asherclarkauthor

I am also on Facebook: @asherclark

You can email me: asherclarkauthor@gmail.com

I will be setting up a website as well.